The Cocaine Princess 6

King Rio

Lock Down Publications and Ca$h
Presents

The Cocaine Princess 6
A Novel by *King Rio*

King Rio

Lock Down Publications
P.O. Box 944
Stockbridge, Ga 30281
www.lockdownpublications.com

Copyright 2022 by King Rio
The Cocaine Princess 6

Lock Down Publications
Like our page on Facebook: Lock Down Publications @
www.facebook.com/lockdownpublications.ldp
Book interior design by: **Shawn Walker**

Stay Connected with Us!

Text **LOCKDOWN** to 22828 to stay up-to-date with new releases, sneak peaks, contests and more…

Thank you!

King Rio

Submission Guideline.

Submit the first three chapters of your completed manuscript to ldpsubmissions@gmail.com, subject line: Your book's title. The manuscript must be in a .doc file and sent as an attachment. Document should be in Times New Roman, double spaced and in size 12 font. Also, provide your synopsis and full contact information. If sending multiple submissions, they must each be in a separate email.

Have a story but no way to send it electronically? You can still submit to LDP/Ca$h Presents. Send in the first three chapters, written or typed, of your completed manuscript to:

LDP: Submissions Dept
P.O. Box 944
Stockbridge, Ga 30281

DO NOT send original manuscript. Must be a duplicate.

Provide your synopsis and a cover letter containing your full contact information.

Thanks for considering LDP and Ca$h Presents.

This book is dedicated to the families of Michael Brown, Eric Garner, and Trayvon Martin.
#ICantBreathe #HandsUpDontShoot

King Rio

Prologue
July 31, 2014
Soldier Field
Chicago, IL

"BULL-ET-FACE! BULL-ET-FACE! BULL-ET-FACE!"

Blake was standing on a circular platform that was set on an electronic timer to make a pneumatic rise to the stage above in less than sixty seconds. He wore loose-fitting black leather Louis Vuitton sweatpants, a million dollar necklace full of 12-carat white diamonds, his half-million- dollar white diamond Hublot watch, and white Louboutin sneakers. Ten- carat whit diamonds were set in his gold earrings and pinkie rings. A Louis Vuitton bandana hung from the cash-filled left pocket of his sweats. Nothing hung from the cash-filled right pocket.

Alexus and the kids stood to his left and Kenneth Lerone, his music manager, was at his right.

"Shut it down out there, Blakey," Alexus said, patting and rubbing his shoulder. "You've got sixty thou-sand fans out there. They paid good money to see you show out tonight. Don't let them down. Do it for the Kings."

Taking a deep breath, Blake tightened his grip on the diamond-encrusted microphone in his hand, clenched his teeth, and kissed his wife's succulent lips.

"I got this, baby," he said. "Just keep the kids close to you. I'll be done with this concert in no time."

"Can we play Monopoly when we get home tonight?" Vari asked. Blake looked down at his eight-year-old daughter and smiled.

"Yeah, Vari, we can play Monopoly. Take your brother over there and sit

down. Keep your brother occupied and I'll get you your own pizza right after the show. Deal?" he asked as he stuck out his hand to shake on it.

Savaria sealed the deal with one hand while balling the collar of King Neal's shirt in the other. "Come on, boy," she said, snatching him along beside her as she dashed toward a row of chairs.

Following another kiss from his wife and a few encouraging words from Kenneth Lerone, Blake stood on the platform and turned into

Bulletface.

The beat to Rick Ross's "War Ready" began booming throughout the stadium. Bulletface had remixed it on his "The Bang Bang Theory" mixtape and it was the song he'd chosen to perform first that night. It was his first day in Chicago since learning of the hit that the Gangster Disciples and Black Disciples had on his head. He wanted to let the people know how he was feeling about the beefs.

War Ready pretty much summed it up.

He closed his eyes for a couple of seconds as the platform rose to the stage above. Then he took two deep breaths and hit the stage flowing.

Fourteen bullets hit me, nigga, fourteen! 47s in my Bugatti, hop out let it ring!

Before dis rap shit all I did was bang and slang Caine I tell my hittas make it rain, they gon make it rain

I spent a million on my chain, nigga, plain Jane Anotha million on my chain, nigga, blang blang

Fuck whatcha heard, we totin' .40s wit dem thirties, nigga Put you in the dirt...now you a dirty nigga

War ready...my shooter wanna gain some stripes

War ready...five racks he'll take ya life

War ready...I got a billion now who wanna fight...

Sudden pandemonium swept through the crowd as Lil Wayne joined Bulletface onstage to perform his featured verse on the remix. More elated screams followed as Rick Ross and Jeezy came out and performed the original version of the song. Bulletface added to the frenzy by throwing thousands of dollars in hundred-dollar bills into the crowd. Then he launched into "By the Corner Store," another track off "The Bang Bang Theory."

I'ma bring somethin' new into town, this Ruger'll pound, P-89 hit you wit a round

But I ain't gotta get stupid and clown, cause my goons stay doin' it and doin' it and doin' it wild

You and ya guy'll two L's, ya bodies catch a few shells, from somethin' in the trunk that stay bangin' like new twelves

Blakey'll hitchoo wit this four-oh boy, and leave you slumped on the front steps at Joe-Joe's door

Listen, you won't win, every time you got a beef wit me, Y'all gon keep on fallin' like Alicia Keys

And I'ma keep on brawlin', just the beast in me, if you thinkin' I'm all cake come get a piece o' me

And I'ma show you you done speculated wrong, on the corner broad day a chrome Tec'll spray ya dome

Niggas on the Ave waitin' for me to call and say it's on, cause when it's on we strap up to infiltrate ya home...yeah

You niggas say y'all want some drama, y'all don't want it, though Catch me wit dat choppa out there trappin' by the corner sto'

Where? By the corner sto', Where? By the corner sto'

Disrespect me they gon find you wet up by the corner sto'...

Bulletface was on fifty, and the show was just beginning. He had more guest appearances lined up. Au-gust Alsina. Rihanna. Kevin Gates. Meek Mill. French Montana, Lil Durk, Yo Gotti, and Rich Home Quan. It would no doubt be an epic night at Soldier Field. He was certain of it.

In the parking lot outside of the stadium, Bulletface's enemies gathered.

King Rio

Chapter 1

'If a nigga want war, I'll catch 'em when I'm on tour I'll blow thirty and this .40, he won't want it no more Bulletface, Bulletface, scream it till ya throat sore

Heard you want some drama, I ain't the nigga you should come for...'

Perspiration lined Bulletface's crisply groomed hairline. He held the diamond-encrusted mic to his mouth, gazing out over the screaming crowd of over sixty thousand fans. His pinkies, wrists, neck, teeth, and earlobes were aglow with over four million in flawless diamonds. Twista, Lil Durk, and Tran and Ceno of Sicko Mobb were pacing the stage with him, anxiously awaiting their verses on "War Time," a track off the "The Bang Bang Theory," Bulletface's platinum-selling mixtape.

He wore an expression of fearlessness. He was a kilo-dealing rap star, a former gunslinger with a history of violence. He was Bulletface, the self-proclaimed King of the Midwest. Though his street beef with several of the Chicago gangs had him more than a little concerned, he was there at Soldier Field as if there was no beef at all.

'...I got me a .50 cal and it's gold-plated wit' a fifty drum in that bitch

I got di foot long and yo' hoe gon' face it till she suck the cum out this dick.

I brought out five mill; make dem strippers love me, walked in the club dey got rich

'Cause we got Money Bagz in this bitch...it's Dub Life in this bitch..."

His torso muscles were bulging, sweaty, and sharply defined. His black Louboutin sneakers were new and spotless. A Louis Vuitton bandana was tied around his left wrist, and the pockets in his baggy black leather sweatpants were full of cash.

Bulletface was on top of the world.

King Rio

He performed five more songs and then brought the show to a close with "My One and Only Love," a song featuring Rihanna that he'd written for his wife, Alexus Costilla.

Alexus and Enrique, her chief of security were waiting with the kids when Blake "Bulletface" King made it backstage.

Enrique spoke gravely as Blake hugged and kissed Alexus. "Chicago police just dispersed the crowd in front of the stadium. There were over a hundred of T-Walk and Chief Keef's guys gathered in the parking lot. They're after you, Blake. Staying here in Chicago isn't safe. They'll be shooting at us every chance they get. Our guys can easily handle them, but we're better off leaving."

"I ain't worried about nothin'," Blake said.

"Well," Alexus said, "you should be. We can stay the night here, but we're leaving first thing in the morning."

Just then, Young Jeezy walked up and slapped a hand onto Blake's shoulder. "After party at Adrian-na's?"

"No," Alexus said quickly, knocking Jeezy's hand away. "He'll be partying with his wife, isn't that right, Mr. King?"

Blake and Jeezy laughed. "I guess so," Blake said, shaking hands with Jeezy.

He bid the other recording artists a goodnight, thanked Tunechi for coming on such short notice, then picked up his sleeping three-year-old son King Neal from a chair and headed out of the stadium. His eight-year-old daughter Savaria and Alexus walked close beside him. A phalanx of armed Costilla Cartel militants disguised as dark-suited bodyguards escorted them to their armored Mercedes Sprinter van. The Bulletface tour bus and two black Escalades – decoy vehicles – pulled off first. The Sprinter, followed by seven white Range Rovers full of bodyguards, took off a moment later.

Settling into his comfortable white leather seat, Blake cast an amorous stare at Alexus. She was sitting across from him, wearing a form- fitting white Chanel dress with matching Louboutin heels. Her thick reddish-brown thighs were shiny with oil. A thin layer of makeup coated her pie-shaped visage. With her exotic features, long black hair, and bountiful derriere, she bore a striking resemblance

14

to urban model Cubana Lust, which is why Blake had chosen the mode to star in his "My one and Only Love" video.

"I know what you're thinking," Alexus said smiling. "You don't know shit," Blake retorted.

"Yes, I do. You want blood. You're thinking about going to war with

T-Walk and Chief Keef." She glanced over at Enrique. "How many of their men have been taken out?"

"Thus far," Enrique hesitated, "somewhere around thirty. Close to fifty others wounded, mostly on Keef's side. Our guys are gearing up for another attack now."

"See?" Alexus said. "Nothing to worry about. Have faith in me. I'll never let you down." She rubbed her belly and smiled.

She was two months pregnant.

King Rio

Chapter 2

They made it to their fifty-million dollar Trump Tower Penthouse without incident. Savaria had fallen asleep during the ride; her pizza plans would have to wait. Blake carried her to bed while Alexus tucked King Neal in.

When he walked in the all-white bedroom he shared with Alexus, she was already showering in the bath-room that was built between their walk-in closets. He undressed hurriedly and joined her in the spacious white marble shower.

"You freaky bastard," she immediately accused.

"What?" he grinned and raised his hands in surrender. "Is it against the law for me to take a shower?"

"You didn't strip that fast just to get in the shower and wash up. I know you, Blake. Nasty ass."

She had her back to him. Clouds of foamy Dove soap were cascading down her body. There were three showerheads, but Blake was content with sharing the one Alexus was using. Gazing at her ample curves, he kissed the nape of her neck, slipped an arm around her waist, and lowered his mouth to her ear.

"You're about to say some freaky shit," she said. His grin burgeoned. "I love you," he said guiltily. "Go ahead. Say what that other head is thinking." "He loves you too."

"I just bet he does."

She turned around and looked at his long ebony pole; it was already growing hard. Her verdant green eyes rose to study his lips, then his eyes.

He pressed his lips against hers and squeezed her ass in his hands. "Let's shower fast," she said.

It took every ounce of restraint he had to hold back. He took what
was probably the quickest shower he'd ever taken, ignoring his smartphone as it began ringing in his pants. Alexus toweled him dry, smiling and shaking her head at his throbbing erection.

Then she squatted down on her haunches and kissed its head, twisting its length in her hands, and smil-ing up at Blake.

His iPhone 5 was still ringing. "Wanna answer that?" Alexus asked. "Fuck that call."

"You sure?"

"Hell yeah. That call can wait. Now, stop teasin' me and get to it."

The majority of his dick disappeared into her mouth, and she pushed it in and out of her throat. She hadn't toweled away the beads of water that covered her flawless body. Blake suddenly decided that she looked better wet. Especially her long, curly, black hair.

She pulled back and ran her tongue along the sides of his rigid pole, licked a droplet of precum from its head, then stood up, gripped his dick in her hand, and pulled him along behind her as she sauntered through his walk-in closet and into their posh white bedroom.

"You lock the door?" she asked, shoving him onto the bed.

He shook his head no and ogled her wobbling derriere as she walked to the door and locked it.

"I don't know if I told you this," she said, crossing the room to the bed, "but I pulled a gun on Porsche the night they shot up your car in New York. I asked her to run me some bath water and the dirty little bitch filled the tub with hot water."

"You had her mom killed," Blake reminded her. "Not on purpose."

"Yeah, but..."

"And it was your fault."

"How you gon' blame me for some shit you did? Blake scooted to the center of the bed, stroking his rock-hard pole.

Sucking her teeth indignantly, Alexus crawled onto the bed, stacked her hands around his strong love muscle, and squeezed it hard. "If you'd keep a lock on this thing, we wouldn't have had to go through that. Oh, I forgot to tell you, our guns arrived while you were performing. A few of

them are here in my closet, and the others are at the Highland Park mansion. And I know where T-Walk's been staying. We'll pay him a visit first thing in the morning."

"I'm shootin' up everything," Blake said tightly.

Alexus slurped him back into her mouth and began slowly sucking, twisting, and turning his length in her hands. He watch in silence for a long while, occasionally thumbing her hair behind her ear to keep it from obstructing his view, and checking his icy gold Hublot watch.

It was 12:40 AM.

There was a wet pop as Alexus sucked the crown of his phallus out of her mouth. She swung a knee over it, positioning herself with her rear facing him, and guided the twelve-inch pole into her warm, snug, juice box.

"I'm feeling brave tonight," she said, looking back at him.

"Yeah?" Blake's signature grin returned.

"Mm hm."

"Well, show me. I wanna see."

He put his hands on her hips and gazed at her undulating ass as she started slamming it down on him, wedging his dick deep inside her with every downward bounce.

By 12:59, his scrotum was tight and his semen was filling her pussy. She curled next to him and fell asleep.

King Rio

Chapter 3

'I'm Bulletface, I'm a bad guy, all da bad bitches wanna be wit' me
I got cocaine by da mountain, nigga, tell da dope boys to come ski
wit' me.

Under my seat where dat heat'll be, thirty round dat's a trilogy
Think I'm Stephen King when I'm in the booth, you should, but this
shit on your TV screens…"

Clad in a black and gold Versace hoody with matching jogging
pants and black Louboutin sneakers, Blake lowered the volume on
"I'm the King," a track off his recently released "The Bang Bang
Theory" mixtape, as he braked to a stop on the corner of 15th and
Trumbull Avenue.

He was driving his matte black armored Bugatti Veyron Super
Sport. The gold-plated .50 caliber Desert Eagle resting on his lap
had red laser sighting and a 50-round drum magazine that was also
gold-plated. The Louis Vuitton duffle bag on the passenger seat
next to him contained

$500,000 in hundred dollar bills, and his gold-plated
Kalashnikov AK-47 was leaning against the duffle, its barrel on the
floor, its equally golden 100- round drum nestled on the edge of the
seat.

A double-stacked Styrofoam full of Lean sat in his cup holder.
The blunt of OG Kush he'd just rolled was stuck between forefinger
and middle finger; smoke curled up in front of his wary brown eyes
as he studied the black Escalade he was parked behind.

According to his blinging Hublot, the time was 2:27 AM. There
were two Apple smartphones on his lap with the golden

Eagle; one of them lit up.

Cup, the chief of the Lawndale neighborhood's Traveling Vice
Lords, was the caller who'd interrupted Blake and Alexus in the
shower, and now he was calling again

Sweeping his eyes around the dark west side street, Blake
answered the call.

"I'm in the 'Lac truck," Cup said. "Don't even bother getting'
out.

Li'l niggas been out here shootin' on sight all month long. The BDs just
shot up my strip club, hit two of my dancers, killed a bouncer, and another chick."

"Was Bubbles in there?"

"Nah. That's why they shot the club up though. Lookin' for her. Tray Savage said she set him up for you that night at the gas station. Sosa took his word and sent some hittas out here."

Blake let out a sigh of relief, glad that Lakita "Bubbles" Thomas had not been a victim in the club shoot-ing. She was one of his exes, and he still had a lot of love for her.

He sipped some Lean as he thought.

Cup said, "I hope you bulletproofed that Bugatti. It's war time out here, young nigga. Ain't nobody safe."

"I'm good," Blake inhaled a mouthful of potent smoke, and looked around for the third time since he'd pulled up. "Is that why you called?"

"Nah."

"What's up?"

"Just follow me. It's about seven blocks from here."

"Hold on a second. My li'l nigga should be pullin' up any…"

Blake paused as he spotted a black Rolls Royce Phantom approaching in his rearview mirror. The Phan-tom belonged to Young Meach, MBM's second biggest rap star, and riding with him were Will Scrill and P.A.T., MBM's other two biggest rap artists.

"A'ight, let's ride," Blake said. He ended the call with Cup and dialed Meach's number as he drove off behind the Escalade.

"Man," Meach said, "on Angela, it damn near went up between us and GBE at Adrianna's. Would've been gunshots if half the Chicago police force didn't show up."

"You know I'm poled up." "Awready."

The Escalade turned into the Trumbull alley. Reluctantly, Blake followed. He sipped more Lean, hit the blunt again, and put it in the ashtray.

"Frenchy brought Khloe to the club wit' him and Durk," Meach continued.

"Was she wearin' somethin' tight?"

"Hell yeah. Ass everywhere, bruh. Lanipop was there too. So many baddies I damn near went crazy. I was on a bad one when the li'l goons got to fightin' wit' GBE. Then the cops came in and shut the club down. Man, we gotta be on the watch for them. You know they ain't playin' no games."

"I'm on the same shit," Blake said.

The Escalade halted at the end of the alley just long enough for two Chicago policemen to walk past, and for a moment, Blake became nervous. Redbone's, Cup's strip club, was to the left at the end of the alley. The club was surrounded by CPD vehicles.

Blake breathed a sigh of relief as the Escalade made a right turn onto 16th Street and led him away from the police.

"They shot up Cup's strip club," Blake said. "Glory Boyz?" Meach asked.

"Yup. Lookin' for Bubbles."

"She got a stupid fat ass too."

"I got her and Shay livin' at my crib in Miami." "And you ain't fuck neither one of 'em?"

"I'm married. Alexus'll kill me."

"Every married nigga we know got a side piece." Blake laughed. "Ain't no bitch worth losin' Alexus."

"Well, give me the key to the Miami mansion. I'll slide through there and get it in."

The sidewalks on both sides of 16th were teeming with young black men and women. The convenience store on Drake was jam-packed. Mostly everyone had their eyes on Blake's multimillion-dollar sports car and Meach's sleek black Phantom.

A girl shouted, "That's Bulletface, y'all!"

Then the Bugatti's powerful W-16 engine propelled the sports car ahead to Millard, where the Escalade turned into another alley and stopped at a garage three houses from the corner.

"You ready?" Meach asked. "Ready for what?" Blake replied. Meach ended the call abruptly.

Tucking the Eagle away in his duffle, Blake took a close look around the alley and pulled the AK-47 onto his lap. He extinguished his blunt in the ashtray. Cup and his partner Li'l Cholly stepped out of the Escalade wearing their usual dapper attire of expensive black business suits with gold ties and pocket squares.

Blake cocked the assault rifle, glanced back at the Phantom, and grinned at the sight of his Money Bagz Management team as they emerged holding black steel AK-47s with dangerously long banana clips.

Aplomb, he pushed the assault rifle's barrel down into his duffle and opened his door. He got out with his Lean in one hand and the heavy duffle bag in the other.

"Can you stay out all night with the dons?" Cup asked Blake. "Nigga, I'm the king. I can do whatever the fuck I wanna do."

"Alexus ain't gon' come and shoot me again, is she? Last time I saw your wife she emptied a .44 in my bulletproof vest, fucked up my nice Italian suit." Cup chuckled and motioned for Blake to follow him through the wrought iron gate next to the garage.

They treaded the well-kept backyard of a three-story red brick building and headed up the walkway to the rear steps. Just as Cup's light- brown hand was turning the knob on the back door, every light in the building seemed to turn on at once.

The door opened.

Blake could not believe his eyes. "Congratulations!" the strippers shouted in unison.

Cup clapped a hand onto Blake's shoulder and gave it a friendly squeeze, smiling widely. "You didn't have a bachelor party before you got married, so we're throwing one for you.""Alexus gon' kill me," Blake muttered.

Chapter 4

Clad in a dark blue Gucci hoody with matching sweatpants and loafers, Trintino "T-Walk" Walkson hopped out of the black minivan with a Tec-9 submachine gun trained on the two black men who were standing on the corner of Trumbull and Douglas Boulevard.

The men had no time to react.

T-Walk shot one of them in the left eye and the forehead, and then put a bullet in the side of the other guy's head. He hurried back into the minivan, and the brawny, dark-skinned man behind the wheel sped off down Douglas.

"GD Folks," the driver said. His nickname was Gusto, a notoriously violent Gangster Disciple from Gary, Indiana.

The man seated next to T-Walk, was Li'l Ant, another GD from Gary, and the other four men were also Gangster Disciples.

"You didn't have to do that shit, fam," Ant said. "That's our job." "Fuck these niggas." T-Walk wiped the gun clean and handed it to

Ant. "On Larry, I'm on killin' every one of them fuck niggas. Blake, Cup,

Li'l Cholly, Meach – all of 'em."

"Yeah, but still, leave the dirty work to us."

"Man," Gusto said, "I want that bitch Alexus. She shot me twice and killed Squirm-G. Wish we could catch her."

They abandoned the minivan on Spaulding. T-Walk's fiancé, Ashley "Thunder" Hunter, was waiting in the driver's seat of his baby blue Range Rover, and Gusto's black Excursion was parked behind it.

T-Walk got in next to Ashley. "Go, baby. Just go," he said, reclining his seat as a CPD cruiser went zip-ping past on Douglas.

"Which way?" Ashley asked nervously. "I don't give a fuck which way you go." "Okay, okay, I'm go-ing."

"Just don't go down Douglas." He flamed up a Newport and looked over at his dark-hued bride to be. Like him, she had her head hidden in a hoody.She rocketed the Range Rover down to 16th Street, made a sharp right turn, and gasped.

T-Walk furrowed his brows. "Oh shit," she said. "What?"

"Cops. A lot of them."

"Shit, take off that hoody," T-Walk said. He saw the flashing lights, and then came the piercing scream of sirens.

"It looks like a club or something. Redbone's," Ashley said. "Some of them are speeding up the alley with their sirens and lights on. We're good. You can look."

She pushed her hoody back, revealing her sexy dark-brown face. MAC was responsible for the shim-mering glossiness of her full lips. The Cowboys fitted cap that was tilted to the right of her head gave her a gangsterish look and T-Walk like it. There were blue diamonds in her gold hoop earrings and rose gold Rolex watch. T-Walk had paid 6.7 million for the 22-carat blue diamond engagement ring she flossed. He'd proposed to her shortly after Alexus, his ex-girlfriend, had caught him cheating on her with Ashley at his Michigan City nightclub. He liked Ashley because, for one, she had an ass like K. Michelle, and for two, she was one of America's most famous reality TV stars.

"What happened?" she asked. "You didn't do anything did you?"

"Nah. My nigga Gusto shot some niggas on Trumbull though." "Well, that explains why the police are speeding up the Trumbull alley."

"I guess it does." "Did he kill them?"

T-Walk shrugged. "I didn't look."

"Gusto scares me. He's too big to be that violent."

"That's my folks." T-Walk looked at the time on his Samsung smartphone and couldn't believe it was already 3:30 AM. "Where are we going now?" Ashley asked.

"Just drive around for a couple more minutes. They say Black came through here in a black Bugatti. Let's see if we can find it."

26

Chapter 5

'I love my big booty bitches, my life a Godfather picture Local club in my city, I fell in love wit' a strip-per.

Bitches know I'm that nigga; I'm talkin' four-door Bugatti I'm tha life of the party; let's get these hoes on a Molly You know I came to stunt, so drop that pussy bitch…'

In Blake's opinion, Maliah and Chyna were the finest steatopygic strippers in America, and seeing their meaty rear cheeks shaking and bouncing in front of him had him on ten. He was making it rain hundred dollar bills on the beautiful dancers. A blunt of OG Kush hung from the corner of his mouth. The tall-backed mahogany and black leather chair he was sitting in was glided with gold. It was the only chair – the only piece of furniture, for that matter, in the black-tiled dining room.

There were eight more strippers. Two of them were sixty-nining on the cash littered floor near the large stereo speakers, which were vibrating with French Montana's "Pop That." The other half-naked dancers were twerking in front of Cup, Li'l Cholly, and the MBM rap artists. Gold bottles of Ace of Spades and thick blunts were in their hands. Smiles were on their faces.

Maliah started giving Blake a lap-dance, facing him. His Versace shirt and hoody were draped over his duffle bag next to the chair, but he still had on his Louis Vuitton bulletproof vest.

"Why'd you have to go and get married?"" Maliah asked. "Do you have any idea how many bad bitches wanna fuck you?"

Chyna leaned in and said, "Girl, this nigga got the biggest dick I've ever seen in my life. Best sex I ever had."

Blake chuckled.

Reaching down between her thighs, Maliah grabbed his dick through his pants and rubbed it tightly. "Oh, my God," she murmured.

"See? It's like a baseball bat, ain't it?" Chyna asked.

Blake grinned and toked on his blunt as Chyna and Maliah began whispering to each other. His dick was brick-hard. In an attempt to keep his mind and eyes off the potential threesome, he glanced across the room at a huge bootied dancer who was staring at him with her hands on her hips.

Her name was Nona Malden. She was his ex-girlfriend.

Maliah said, "Bulletface, can we take you in one of these bedrooms and have some real fun?" She stood up, wrapping her fingers around his wrist, and tried to pull him to his feet.

He didn't budge.

"Come on, Bulletface," Chyna urged, pulling on his other arm.

Just then, an empty Hennessey bottle crashed through the living room window.

Chapter 6

"What the fuck?" Blake said. The men retrieved their weapons.

Blake snatched his gold-plated assault rifle out of the duffle bag.

"Hold on a second," Cup said, frowning quizzically as he dialed a number on his smartphone.

The strippers were already putting on their clothes and scooping the hundreds from the floor. Blake ogled their gelatinous lady lumps, and then shifted his attention to the shattered living room window.

A light-skinned man who'd been asleep on the sofa was now standing at the window. He seemed to be around Blake's age. He was just as muscular as Blake was, and he had thick, cornrowed braids running from the front of his scalp to the nape of his neck. The butt of a pistol hung over the side of his baggy jeans.

"Who is that?" Blake asked no one in particular.

Nona walked up beside Blake. "That's my brother Biggs. He just got out the Feds last night. We got drunk before you got here and he passed out on us. He's a Vice Lord too, grew up with the Unknowns on Washington and Kostner."

Just then, Cup ended the call, shook his head, and turned to Blake. "I had some young niggas watchin' the block but the law rode through a couple minutes ago and scared 'em off. They saw a black Expedition pull up right before they left."

Biggs pointed out the window. "Shit, that's a black Expedition right there. It's parked down the street."

Nona said, "One of them bad ass kids threw that bottle. Y'all know how it is out here."

"We'll go out the front and see what's up wit' that Expedition," Meach said. "Blake, you go out the back."

Nodding his head in agreement, Blake put on his shirt and hoody and had Nona grab his duffle. Meach and the other MBM members headed out the front door with their assault rifles in hand. Biggs fell in step beside Blake as Cup, Li'l Cholly, and the strippers preceded them to the back door.

Biggs let out a funny sounding laugh. "How in the hell did you get a gold AK?" When he got no reply, he said, "My nigga Li'l Lord used to talk about you all the time. Said he was proud of you."

The name Li'l Lord got Blake's attention. Li'l Lord was serving time in Indiana State Prison for a murder he'd committed back in 2005. He was a stomp-down TVL who'd been born there in the Lawndale neigh-borhood under Cup's tutelage before moving to Blake's hometown in northwest Indiana; he was a dope boy and a Dub Life Goon who'd taught Blake how to cook cocaine into crack, how to fight, and the value of the truth. Black looked up to Li'l Lord, loved him like a brother.

"I holla at my nigga all tha time," Blake said.

Biggs nodded and drew a Glock from his hip as they exited the back door and descended the three con-crete stairs. His eyes darted in every direction, as did Blake's.

"I met that nigga in the county," Biggs said. "He was droppin' muhfuckas, wasn't he?"

"On Vice Lord," Biggs laughed, nodding again. "Bruh beat up every fuck nigga in the cellblock." "That's all he used to do."

"Yeah. He done calmed down now. Heard he writin' books now, on some Donald Goines type shit."

"I just want bruh to get out and spend some of this money wit' me.

Hate they got my nigga locked up like that. It's been almost nine years."

"He'll be out in a couple more years," Biggs said as they made it to the Bugatti.

Blake popped the trunk and had Nona drop his duffle bag inside it.

She had a sour look on her face, and he figured he knew what it was all about. He'd ended their relation-ship abruptly and without any reason other than the fact that he loved fucking the dime piece groupies who were always waiting backstage after his shows. Then he'd rekindled his relationship with Alexus, and now they were happily married.

Blake decided that Nona had a right to be upset.

The other steatopygic dancers sauntered off to a blacked-out party bus further up the alley, chatting about getting a suite at the Hilton. Cup and Cholly climbed in the Escalade.

"Love your music," Biggs said. "It's all we bumped up in the Feds. I got a mixtape I'm about to drop soon as I get it recorded. Gon' have bruh on the intro."

Blake nodded. "Take down my number and hit me up tomorrow. I'm ask bruh about you."

"I'm certified. You can ask every real Lord in the Feds, from KT to T-Fly and everybody else."

KT (King Tray) was the leader of the Mafia Insane Vice Lords, and T-Fly was a high-ranking Traveling Vice Lord. Blake had learned about them years prior when he first became a TVL.

"You on your feet? Got some bread?" Blake asked, scrutinizing Biggs and ignoring Nona's belligerent stare.

"I'm good," Biggs said. "Sis gave me fifty racks. I'ma grab me a Chevy and a whole shirt, bounce all the way back. Shouldn't take me no longer than a..."

Biggs was silenced by a stentorian burst of fully automatic gunfire. The luminous shots brought light to the dark street out front.

Blake snatched the golden Eagle out of his duffle bag and closed the trunk. Biggs was already in the pas-senger seat when Blake got in and started the engine.

He made a U-turn and followed the Escalade and the party bus onto 16th Street. The gunfire stopped just as suddenly as it started.

The party bus turned left and raced away.

Blake made a right and braked behind the Escalade. He wedged his AK-47 between his seat and the door and waited for Meach's sleek black Phantom to come veering out of the alley. When it did, Scrill's bald brown head was hanging out the passenger window.

"Meet up at the Trump?" Scrill shouted, ducking back into the window as Meach veered left and sped off down 16th.

Blake swerved around Cup's SUV and stomped down on the gas pedal, lurching the Bugatti forward. He turned left and crossed Douglas Boulevard to Roosevelt Road in a matter of seconds. He was making a swift right turn onto Roosevelt when his iPhone 5 rang.

He half expected that it was either Meach, Scrill, or Cup calling, but a quick look at the smartphone proved him wrong on every guess.

It was his wife, the beautiful African American and Mexican queen of the underworld. They FaceTimed.

Alexus Costilla's face was a sleepy, petulant scowl.

"I'm fucking you up, Black," she said. She was sitting up in bed with the lamp on. "Where are you?"

Blake grinned. "On my way home now, baby." "Where'd you go?"

"Cup called me."

"The hell's that supposed to me?"

"I love you." His gleaming diamond grin widened into a full-on smile. "Well, I came out here to catch up with all them fuck-niggas who came to my concert talkin' war. You know I'm on that. They shot up Cup's strip club, killed a bouncer, and some girl, and shot two dancers. I just passed Douglas and it looked like another murder scene, buncha cops, and yellow tape on Trumbull. And I'm pretty sure somebody just got whacked on Millard."

"Jesus Christ." Alexus shook her head and rubbed her eyes. She stared at him for a brief moment, and then regarded him with a dubious squint. "What was that sneaky little smile about?"

The sneaky little smile returned. "Don't play with me Blake."

"I love you."

"I'll cut it off," Alexus threatened.

"I ain't did nothin'," Blake said with a guilty chuckle. "Cup threw me a bachelor party since I didn't have one before the wedding. I got a few lap dances and tossed some bands but that's it, I swear."

"A few lap dances. Hmm." "It wasn't—"

"No, no, no," Alexus said quickly. "I'll tell you what. When you get home, lay on the couch, and let your lap make love to that leather since you seem to enjoy lap dances so much. And if I find out you stuck your dick in one of those…"

Suddenly, Biggs shoved a hand against Blake's shoulder and pointed at a blue Range Rover and a minivan that had just pulled up alongside the Bugatti. They were at a red light on Roosevelt and Kedzie.

The minivan's sliding door rolled open, and out leapt three gunmen. They opened fire on the Bugatti.

King Rio

Chapter 7

Blake immediately locked the doors.

Biggs raised his gun to return fire, but Blake pushed the gun down and gave the shooters a gelid stare. Their bullets were pounding into the thick glass of Blake's bulletproof window. He'd dropped his smartphone to the floor; Alexus was shouting his name repeatedly.

"This muhfucka bulletproof?" Biggs said in disbelief. "Pull off!" Calmly shaking his head, Blake handed his Desert Eagle to Biggs,

pulled the gold-plated AK-47 onto his lap, and waited for the thunderous gunfire to cease.

The Range Rover turned left and sped off down Kedzie. Then the shooters rushed back into the minivan.

An expansive smile crossed Blake's face.

"My turn now," Blake said, pushing open his door with the AK-47 aimed at the minivan. He squeezed the trigger, and Biggs started shooting too.

The minivan hardly made it across Kedzie.

King Rio

Chapter 8

"I'm sick of Blake," Alexus said, twirling a curlicue of her long curly black hair around an index finger and gazing vacantly at the 100-inch flat screen television across the room from her.

She was bundled in a thick white Chanel robe on the sumptuous white Italian leather sofa in the living room of her top floor Trump Tower penthouse. Tears were streaming down from her worried green eyes. Her half-sister Mercedes was seated to the left of her, wrapped in an equally thick black Gucci robe.

Porsche, Mercedes's younger sister, was sitting on her boyfriend Tone's lap in an easy chair.

They were awake at 4:30 in the morning watching ABC7 News, and the top story was about Chicago's gun violence...and how billionaire gangsta rapper Bulletface's car had been found on Roosevelt Road with over fifty bullets embedded in its armored exterior. Further down Roosevelt, a gray minivan was found with twice as many bullet holes.

The three black men inside the minivan had not survived the shooting. Neither had the two men who'd been shot in their heads on the corner of Douglas and Trumbull, and the two men in the Ford SUV next to Shirley Earl High School on 16th and Millard.

"I wonder why he ain't called yet," Porsche said, extending her fingers to glance at her perfectly mani-cured nails. The tips of them were painted pink. Her Chanel halter and boy shorts were the same color, accentuating her rich dark skin.

Alexus shook her head. "I don't know if I should be mad or worried. This bastard went out and had a bachelor party. We both agreed not to have bachelor and bachelorette parties."

"Well," Mercedes said, "have a bachelorette party."

"I'll plan it!" Porsche said excitedly. Then she scoffed, "We don't even know if your husband is still alive and we're-"

"Shut up, Porsche." Mercedes offered her little sister a frigid stare. "Blake is fine. I'm sure he'll be walk-ing through that door any minute now."

The mere notion of Blake being dead thickened the stream of tears that were still cascading down Alex-us's pretty face. She picked up her smartphone and Googled 'Bulletface' to see what the media had to say about Blake.

Chicago police disperse crowds of angry gangsters at Bulletface concert; rapper's Bugatti later found riddled with bullets on city's west side – TMZ.com

Chief Keef warns Bulletface to stay out of Chicago via Twitter; Bulletface ignores threat and ends up with a car full of bullets – KollegeKidd.com

Alexus shuddered and pulled her knees up to her chest.

Just then, the door to the penthouse opened, and Blake swaggered in with a handsome brown-skinned man at his side.

Alexus felt her heart swell in her chest as she jumped up and ran to Blake. She fell into his arms, wrapped her thick legs around his waist, and pressed her lips to his.

"I'm good, baby," he said, squeezing her ass and sucking her lower lip into his mouth.

"Are you okay?" she asked, drawing back to study his handsome black face.

"Yeah, I'm Louis Ball," he said, entering the living room. "Niggas shot the Bugatti up. Cops questioned me. I ain't know nothin'. You know I ain't goin'."

His veiny black hands roamed her thick derriere as she buried her face in the crook of his neck. Her an-ger of the impromptu bachelor party was gone. She was just glad that he hadn't been hurt.

"Who's your friend?" Mercedes asked.

"Biggs," said the brawny young man. "My name's Biggs." He set the duffle bad he was holding down on the white marble floor and turned to Blake. "I'm about to go and get a room, bruh. I'm too tired."

Alexus drew back, lowered her feet to the floor, and watched Blake shake his head no.

"Mercedes, let him sleep in your bed," he said.

Mercedes smiled suggestively as she stood and led Biggs to her bedroom. Gazing into Blake's eyes, Alexus kissed his lips again.

Then she caught a whiff of an unfamiliar perfume, and her anger returned.

She crossed her arms over her chest and squinted.

Blake chuckled, grinned, and picked up his duffle bag. "Can I please get some sleep before I get cussed out?"

"Oh, now you want some sleep. Your ass wasn't trying to sleep at that bachelor party."

"You act like I planned it."

"I don't give a damn who planned it. Keep on playing with me, Blake. Keep fucking around and see what happens."

Blake started off toward the bedroom, and Alexus was hot on his trail.

She sucked her teeth. "I hope you know that I'm not done with you.

I'll let you sleep, but please believe this isn't over." He didn't respond.

"Black bastard. I wish they would've shot your dumb ass."

Blake walked in their bedroom, kicked off his sneakers, and turned to face Alexus. His signature grin irritated her.

"I should slap that stupid little grin right off your face. Asshole." "Why would you wanna slap your husband?"

"Don't fucking play with me, Blake."

"I ain't playin'. I'm serious." He stripped down to his boxers, yawned, and smiled.

"Let me smell your dick," Alexus said, squatting before him and yanking down his black Versace box-ers.

He laughed as his flaccid penis fell free. Alexus moved forward and sniffed. Satisfied, she stood and put her hands on her hips.

"Am I good?" he asked, pulling up his boxers. "For now you are."

"I wouldn't cheat on you, baby. Never. I love you too much." "Sure you do."

"I do," he persisted.

"Mm hmm. Whatever. What the hell happened to your car?" "The fuck you think happened? Chiraq happened." Blake climbed into bed and started taking off his jewelry, placing each piece on his nightstand. "I was on my way home, talkin' to you. Some niggas pulled up in a minivan and hopped out shootin'."

Alexus closed and locked the bedroom door, keeping a keen eye on Blake in hopes of possibly glimps-ing a non-verbal admission of guilt. She dropped her robe over the arm of the sofa at the foot of their bed and slipped under the covers next to Blake in her white-lace Chanel teddy.

Blake turned toward her, ginning even wider than before.

"They say married couples should never go to bed mad at each other," he said, his right hand sliding up between her legs.

She snapped her thighs shut. Blake's grin burgeoned.

"Too bad I'm already awake," Alexus said with a smile of her own.

She grabbed the Kindle Fire tablet from her nightstand and turned it on. "I'm actually glad you got me up this early. I can finish reading Shan's newest book and start on Terry McMillan's before the kids wake up. Oh, and our new iPhone 6s are here."

"I don't give a fuck about no iPhone." Blake moved in for a kiss, forcing two fingers between her thighs and attacking her clitoris through the soft fabric of her teddy.

Alexus bobbed away from the kiss, and his lips found her neck. She tried to push the invasive hand away, but his relentless fingertips continued their rough assault.

Her mouth fell open, and she sucked in a breath. His lips pecked at her neck, her shoulder, the swell of her breasts. Then his head slipped beneath the covers, and his kisses took the place of those unrelenting fingertips.

Alexus wanted to deny him the goodies in response to the bachelor party he'd attended, but the goodies didn't want him to stop. She failed to resist as he peeled off her teddy and went back to kissing and licking on her favorite spot to be kissed and licked.

She laid her Kindle tablet on the nightstand and thumbed the covers up and over Blake's head so she could admire his flickering tongue. He smiled up at her, and she couldn't tell if it was a guilty smile or an innocent one.

head.

"You're so stupid," Alexus said, laughing softly and shaking her.

"You love me though," Blake said.

"Just as much as I hate you." She tried laughing again but it came out as a cotton moan. Gripping his short crop of wavy black hair in the palms of her hands, she began winding her hips.

A steady hum of fluctuating moans ensued.

Blake's cunnilingus skills were so well honed that it took him less than three minutes to bring Alexus to a breathtaking orgasm.

Her body tensed. Her midsection quaked. Orgasmic juices gushed out of her, and Blake greedily tongued it all into his mouth.

Rising up on his knees, Blake whipped out his twelve-inch love muscle and eased it into her juicy pussy.

Alexus forgot all about the bachelor party.

King Rio

Chapter 9

She had not planned to go back to sleep, but Blake's good loving was the best cure for insomnia.

A knock at the bedroom door awakened her.

"Momma." It was Savaria, Blake's daughter from a previous relationship.

With a groggy sigh, Alexus slipped out of bed, picking up her smartphone, and checking the time as she went to the door.

7:14 a.m.

She unlocked the door and opened it a crack.

Vari's pretty brown face was half-hidden behind her curly brown hair, but her smile was clearly visible.

"What it is it, Vari?" Alexus asked.

"Can you wake up my daddy so I can ask him something?"

"Go ahead," Alexus said, opening the door and smiling innocently.

She went to the foot of the bed, put on her robe, and watched as Vari grabbed her daddy's should in both hands and shook him awake.

His sleepy eyes opened slowly. He squinted and blinked at Savaria. Alexus laughed.

"Daddy, can I go to the OMG Girls concert?"

Blake drew back in disbelief. "Are you serious? You woke me up to ask me that?"

"Yes." Vari clasped her hands together pleadingly. She was an eight- year-old who knew how to get her way.

"I'll tell you what," Blake said. "If you make sure nobody wakes me up until twelve o'clock, you can go, and if you ain't outta here in five seconds, I'm changing my mind."

"Can my cousins –" "One."

"-Tiff and Daniella take me?" "Two."Vari sucked her teeth and smiled. "Love you, Daddy." She kissed Blake on the cheek and ran from the room.

King Rio

Just then, Alexus's handsome chief of security, Enrique Aleman, appeared in the doorway. His black Hartmarx suit was impeccable, and it matched his expensive sunglasses.

"Morning, boss lady," he said. "Got a minute?"

Alexus nodded and stepped out into the hallway with him.

He had two iPhone 6 Plus smartphones in his hand. He gave them to Alexus, and she studied them for a moment.

"Signal scramblers have already been installed," Enrique said. "Apple requested that we keep them out of the public's eye until they're revealed on September ninth. Go to YouTube and type in I-S-I-S. ISIS."

"That terrorist group in Iraq?"

Enrique nodded somberly. "You can't get a break, kid. The guy who's been beheading the Yazidis and sending them fleeing up that mountain. He's the main executioner of ISIS – well, he was. Now he's some-where in Central America. No one knew of his whereabouts until four hours ago when entire cities in Panama, Costa Rica, Honduras, and El Salvador were seized by tens of thousands of armed men who claim to be a new branch of ISIS. Newly converted Muslims. They've taken control of military weapons and vehicles. They're beheading police and soldiers and slaughtering every man, woman, and child who refuses to convert."

Alexus gasped as she began reading the video descriptions.

'Hundreds, perhaps thousands, slaughtered in the streets of Central America; sudden uprising of Central American ISIS faction to blame...'

'Military bases in Panama, Honduras, and El Salvador overrun by ISIS militants in early-morning at-tacks...'

The description of another video made Alexus cringe.

'In this five minute ISIS video, three men believed to be members of the Los Zetas drug cartel are brutal-ly beheaded after executioner rants against "Mexico's cocaine queen"...'

Enrique said, "You wouldn't believe me if I told you this guy's name."

"What's his name?" Alexus asked. She wasn't sure if she wanted to hear the answer.

44

"Juan Donald Costilla."

"He's named after my father? Oh, God, please don't tell me he's my brother."

"No. he's the grandson of your grandfather's brother. I looked into it. His father named him after Papi. He grew up in Panama City, traveled to Yemen in oh-four as a journalist, and ventured off into Mosul Province in Iraq. I believe that's when he secretly joined the Sunni extremists who are now known as ISIS."

"Okay." Alexus shrugged. "He's a distant family member. What does any of this have to do with me?"

"His parents were killed by the Sinaloa cartel a few years ago, and now he's somehow found out that you're the top boss of the Mexican drug trade. I think Jenny put him on your trail. He's given his ISIS fighters strict instructions to kill every drug cartel member they encounter. They plan to destroy every drug pusher in Mexico."

Alexus nodded thoughtfully. "And they're heading toward Mexico." "Seems like it."

"Call the Setas, the Simaloas, the Gulfs, and our men. I want five thousand men on the southern border of Mexico."

"We have a hundred and seventy thousand guns; we can send a helluva lot more than five thousand men." Enrique put a hand on Alexus's should and gave it a gentle squeeze. "I'll take care of it. I'm gonna call Pedro and give him the orders. No worries."

"Don't let them fuck up my money, Enrique." "Trust me; you have nothing to worry about." Alexus didn't agree.

King Rio

Chapter 10

In the bathtub, Alexus soaked and listened to some Mary J. Bilge while she ruminated over the ISIS situation, Blake's beefs with Chicago's ruthlessly murderous Gangster Disciples and Black Disciples, and the baby that was growing in her belly.

She was the CEO of Costilla Corp., which owned the number one television network in the entertain-ment industry. She was the boss of the Costilla Cartel, a conglomerate of Mexican drug cartels that now included the Los Zeta Cartel, the Sinaloa Cartel, and the Gulf Cartel. Her cartel was raking in well over 1.5 billion a month is drug sales, and she had over 70 billion in dirty money piled atop wooden pallets at "The Money Mansion," a sprawling hilltop mansion she owned in Malibu, California.

Bottom line, she had more than enough money and power to fend off ISIS and Blake's enemies. She just had to keep Blake out of the streets until their foes were eliminated.

Alexus sighed and sank deeper into the white marble tub. Maybe the child that had been growing inside her for the past two months would keep her husband in the house after his shows, but she doubted it. The streets loved Bulletface, and Bulletface loved the streets. He was a thuggish sex symbol to millions of women, especially the black girls in ghettos all across the country; he was idolized by dope boys and gangsters from New York to Los Angeles and everywhere in between.

Rubbing a hand up and down her belly, Alexus wondered if she was having a boy or the daughter, she'd always dreamed of having. She certainly didn't want another son; her three-year-old son King Neal Costilla was a handful, and she couldn't fathom raising a second boy.

Out of the corner of her eye, she spotted Porsche rummaging through her massive walk-in closet.

"Lexi, can I wear a pair of yo' white Louboutin pumps?"

"Thanks for asking before you just go picking through my closet," Alexus said, her tone full of sarcasm.

Porsche stepped into the bathroom with her hands on her hips and a smirk on her face. She sucked her teeth.

"Don't do me, Lexi."

"Don't go in my closet without asking."

"Okay, okay. Shit." Porsche rolled her eyes. "Girl, have you been on Twitter this morning'? They goin' ham about Bulletface getting' his car shot up last night."

"Why would I wanna see that?"

"Uh, I don't know, maybe because he's your husband. I mean, you did marry the nigga. And you can quit comin' at me with that li'l pregnancy attitude. I didn't knock you up," she said with another suck of the teeth and roll of the eyes. "Anyways…it is Friday, the first of the month. Gon' be ninety-four degrees outside. Ain't no better day to have a bachelorette party."

The notion brought a conspirational smile to Alexus's face. Casting a thoughtful glance at her new smartphone, she said, "I had forgotten all about that."

"Well, I sho in the hell didn't forget. I'm ready to turn the fuck up. Mandingos for everybody. Let me set it up. Please let me set it up. We'll have the best day ever, I promise."

Porsche clasped her hands together pleadingly and put on her most luminous smile. Then her eyes moved to the smartphone Alexus was holding, and her expression turned sour.

"What in the hell is that?" "The new iPhone 6 Plus." "How'd you get it already?" "I have my ways/"

"Well, why didn't I get one? I bet Blake got one."

Beaming Alexus thumbed her way to Instagram and uploaded a photo she'd snapped at Blake's concert the night before. It was a rearview picture of Blake and August Alsina on stage with thousands of smartphone cameras flashing in the crowd before them.

Seconds later, the photo had over twenty thousand likes.

"Wheel in one of my suitcases," Alexus said, uploading a second photo of herself with Blake and Rihan-na backstage.

Each of the four white Chanel suitcases in her closet contained five million in bank-new hundred-dollar bills. Porsche rolled one into the bathroom and zipped it open.

"You should put locks on these suitcases. This is way too much money," Porsche suggested, lifting out one of the ten-thousand dollar bundles and fanning through it. "What am I supposed to do with this money? Don't send me on no dummy missions."

"Get yourself a room, call all the male strip clubs, and have their best men come to audition. Give them a grand apiece for the audition and whoever's selected for the bachelorette party will get fifty grand apiece when it's over."

Porsche shook her head in disagreement. "We should fly to Vegas." "Either we do it my way or we don't do it at all."

"You are the biggest bitch I know."

"Thank you." Alexus smiled. "Take a hundred grand for now, and use some of it to buy your own shoes."

With another suck of the teeth, Porsche took nine more cash bundles out of the suitcase and left out mut-tering something under her breath.

Alexus finished bathing and got out of the tub with a mind full of lascivious thoughts. Toweling off, she envisioned her fingertips traversing down the oily mountain and valleys of a male stripper's abdomen. She imagined him to be tall and dark, like Blake, only with cornrows and sexy hazel eyes.

She squeezed her eyes shut, forcing away the arousing vision as she pulled on a snow-white Chanel jumpsuit. She studied herself for a brief moment in her closet's gold-framed mirror. Her baby bump was hardly visible. Her vivid green eyes were bright and pretty, and her derriere was just as large and round as it had been the day she'd met her husband.

"Yes," she said finally. "I'm still the baddest."

A confident smile grew on her face, and then she received a chilling phone call that stole hear confidence like a thief in the night.

King Rio

Chapter 11

"Hello, is this Alexus Costilla?"

"It's Alexus Costilla-King now, but yes." "This is FBI Special Agent Josh Sneed—" "I know who you are."

"Okay, well…I've got bad news."

Sneed took a deep breath and let it out slowly. He was standing outside the front doors of the Minority Television Network tower, which was just across the street from the Trump International Hotel and Tower where Alexus and her family resided. There were fourteen more plainclothes FBI agents on the already busy downtown street, their eyes flicking vigilantly in every direction.

"Have you seen the news this morning? Sneed asked, lighting a Marlboro and tightly eyeing a Hispanic man who was pulling up in a BMW convertible.

"Yeah, I've seen it," Alexus said. "An ISIS group in Central America right?"

"Yes. They plan to destroy the drug cartels and attack the United States. At least that's what their social media accounts are claiming. Our sources are saying they have somewhere in the neighborhood of fifteen thousand armed fighters, but we believe there are a lot more. Most of them are people who've lost friends and family members to the violence of drug cartels."

"My question is how did all this happen overnight?"

"They kept it under wraps. I'm guessing they were using coded messages through the mail, no phone calls, or emails. The President and his team are on a video conference with Congress as we speak. He'll be addressing the nation shortly. Drones have been deployed to watch over the situation. More than likely, we'll be seeing air strikes in the coming days.

The terror attacks we suffered at the hands of your aunt Jenny have instilled enough fear in our govern-ment. They'll act immediately on this ISIS threat. Especially after word is spread of the threat we intercepted this morning regarding you."

Sneed paused for affect. He heard Alexus sigh through the phone.

King Rio

The Chicano in the BMW seemed to be texting someone on his own smartphone. Sneed looked further down the street at a non-descript white van that was full of heavily armed FBI agents. He was grateful for their presence. He never felt safe anywhere near Alexus Costilla.

"What threat?" she asked.

"As I'm sure you know, the MS-13 street gang originated in El Salvador. Many of the gang's bosses are still there. They send orders to their underbosses her in the States, and those orders are then passed on to their foot soldiers." He took another dramatic pause, but only long enough to inflate his lungs with a soothing billow of smoke. "We believe MS-13's top boss has converted to ISIS. A call from him to an underboss was intercepted about an hour ago. He told the guy to ambush your security team and kill you, and to behead you if possible. It's supposed to go down sometime this morning. Wish I knew when, but no exact time was given. We've got twelve undercover vehicles on Wabash Avenue alone, with twenty more in the area. Two dozen agents in the Trump building, twenty in your network's tower across the street, and I've got fourteen of my best men standing out here with me. Got two drones in the sky, snipers three blocks down, two Special Weapons and Tactics teams. You ain't got much to worry over, but this extra security will cost you an extra dime or two."

Alexus went silent; then said, "No problem. I'll foot the bill. I'm pretty sure my men can handle it, but there's no such thing as too much security. Thanks for the heads up."

The call was ended, and Sneed smoked his cigarette and waited.

Chapter 12

Clad in a black sports bra with matching leggings and Nike running shoes, Alexus's mother was jogging on the treadmill in her top-floor office at the MTN Tower. Her computer tablet was propped up in front of her; on its screen, Joel Osteen's latest biblical lesson was playing, and he had Rita Mae Bishop's full attention.

As President of MTN, COO of Costilla Corp., and host of the most- watched daytime talk show on tele-vision, Rita's weekdays were an endless schedule of meetings and interviews. Her morning jobs and Osteen's preaching gave her the energy she needed to make it through the days, and she had made it down to her target weight of 155 pounds.

Her tight schedule also served a purpose; it kept her from thinking about the fact that her daughter was a Mexican drug cartel boss.

She'd learned of it from their family therapist, and now she believed it to be true. Now all the assassina-tion attempts on Alexus made sense. Now the source of her daughter's fifty-billion-dollar inheritance was obvious.

Though Alexus had yet to admit to her role in the underworld, Rita knew what was going on, and she prayed about it often.

At exactly 10:30 a.m., Rita aborted the treadmill and bent over next to it, hands on her knees, perspiration dripping from her dark brown face.

She downed a bottle of ice-cold water and toweled off the sweat just as the phone on her polished oak desk rang. She picked up the phone and it was Princess Spaulding, her secretary.

"Attorney Bostic's here to see you. Hair and makeup stylists are on their way up. Tyler Perry called. So did Loni Love."

"Loni Love?" Rita was unfamiliar with the name.

"She's one of the hosts on "The Real," a new talk show on Fox. It'll be premiering soon. An all-female roundtable. They're asking to come on your show to promote "The Real." Tamar Braxton is also one of the hosts."

"Send in Bostic."

Rita hung up and headed into her custom-designed bathroom. It boasted a glassed-in shower, two small closets, and a four-seat Jacuzzi that had not yet been used. She stripped down, stepped into the shower, turned on the water, and adjusted it to a fairly cool temperature. She was lathering up when she heard her office door opening.

"I'm in here, Britney." Rita slid the glass door shut and touched a button on the wall that fogged the glass just as Britney Bostic's silhouette appeared.

Of the tens of thousands of Americans on the Costilla Corp. payroll, Rita considered the charismatic young lawyer her favorite. Britney Bostic was a strong black woman who reminded Rita of herself when she was twenty years younger.

"I don't know what's going on," Britney said, "but you've got about triple the number of bodyguards you usually have waiting out in the reception area, there's armed security on every floor and elevator, and that FBI agent who used to look after Alexus is standing out front. I don't know if it has anything to do with Blake being shot at last night or what."

"As long as Jenny Costilla hasn't risen from the dead, I'm fine."

"Forbes just released its list of the four hundred richest Americans.

"Is Alexus number one?"

"No, she's number three. They have her listed as having a net worth of 58 billion. Warren Buffett's right in front of her with 67 billion and Bill Gates is number one with 81 billion. Can you believe he and his wife have given away 35 billion since 1992? He just donated 50 billion to help fight that Ebola outbreak in Africa." Two seconds later she added, "You're number ninety-nine with 7 billion.

Rinsing the foamy shampoo from her hair, Rita took a moment to absorb the staggering sum of her net worth. Never in a million years would she have imagined herself having so much wealth. Growing up in Baton Rouge, Louisiana, she had lived a sheltered, Christian way of life in a dilapidated low-income African American neighborhood, and she'd been just as poor as everyone else. Now she and her daughter were two of the wealthiest people in America.

"The reality of all that money is overwhelming, isn't it?" Britney asked, reading Rita's mind. "I know the feeling. I cleared over 200 million after taxes when we sold the clothing line. Things immediately changed.

Suddenly, it was up to me to employ and support all my family and friends. Every person I've ever met started calling me, inboxing me on Facebook, following me on Twitter. It got crazy fast."

Rita opened the shower door a crack and had Britney hand her a bath towel while she turned off the wa-ter. "With great wealth comes great responsibility," she said, drying off. "It's a blessing from God to be able to help others. Sometimes all the attention gets to me too, but the opportunity to give back makes it all worthwhile."

"It certainly does," Britney agreed.

Wrapping herself in the towel, Rita got out of the shower, disappeared into her shoe closet, and emerged moments later wearing a light gray Pucci tube dress and black and gray Louboutin heels. She went to her desk and sat down in her leather swivel chair.

"Did you see the news about ISIS?" Britney asked. "I caught a few minutes of it."

"People are worried they might make it into Mexico and cross the border into the U.S."

"Nothing can be worse than Jenny was. And my daughter's security team is pretty efficient. They've got more than enough firepower to hold off attacks. Then we'll fly off to that island I bought near Barbados."

"You bought an island?"

"Right after I recuperated from being nailed to that cross," Rita said with a nod. She opened her bottom desk drawer and lifted out a black steel Tec-9 submachine gun with a 50-round clip attached to its underside. "I bought this, too," she added, and laid the gun down on her desk. "I've done a lot of target practice with this gun. Had a shooting range constructed on the island, at the far end of a landing strip for our planes. It's a nice little getaway. I named it Nevaeh. Cost me a quarter billion altogether, but I definitely got my money's worth. There's a three-story mansion made of steel and glass, a bomb-resistant underground bunker, five watchtowers, four airplane hangars. It's the safest home we have."

Britney settled into the black leather chair across from Rita, gazing at the smartphone in her hand. She was slender, dark, and stunning in a cherry-red pantsuit and heels.

"In the ISIS video that shows three alleged cartel members being beheaded, the killer said, and I quote, 'Let this be a message to the cocaine queen. Your drug wars have devastated our community for years, and now, we are striking back. You and your drug dealing thugs will face the wrath of the Islamic State, in the name of our great prophet Jennifer Costilla.'"

Rita's mouth fell open. "No," she said. "They consider Jenny a martyr?"

"Apparently so."

"So who's the cocaine queen?"

Britney rolled her eyes and said nothing. Rita bowed her head and prayed.

Chapter 13

King of the whole thing; fuck whoever steppin' up Bulletface the king, I'm number one you niggas sec-ond up L's up for dem hittas, if ya feel me hold ya weapons up

.40s wit dem thirties, pussy nigga yeah we weaponed up –

Porsche ducked just in time, and the pillow went sailing over her head. It struck her sister's bedroom door as she was closing it. She laughed, pushing down from her ears the pink-diamond-encrusted Beats headphones that were plugged into her iPhone 5.

She'd been rapping along to "King," the first track on Bulletface's yet-to-be-released "Took the Throne" album.

"Watch your mouth in front of these kids," Mercedes chastised. She was sitting on the foot of her bed, clipping King Neal's fingernails as he stood silently between her parted legs.

Savaria was busy playing a word game on her smartphone on the other side of the bed, and the hugely muscled man who'd introduced himself as Biggs was asleep in the middle of the bed.

"That was Bulletface in the truth," Porsche said, her voice replete with excitement. "Name another rap star nigga who's still heavy in the streets like he is wit' all dat money. He done had three Bugattis get shot up in the past few years alone, and he still ain't stopped droppin' music. I swear; if that nigga wasn't married to Alexus I'd be all on his sexy ass."

Vari regarded Porsche with a look of disgust. "My daddy don't like you like that."

Mercedes cracked up laughing, and King Neal joined in the laughter for the heck of it.

Rolling her eyes, Porsche went to the computer desk in the far right corner of the room, took a seat, and logged into Facebook. "Alexus just gave me the money to pay for the bachelorette party. I'm about to go online and look for some strippers." She glanced at Vari and King and added, "Dancers, I mean."

"You meant strippers," Vari said without looking up from her iPhone. "I know what a stripper is. They're all on YouTube.""Did

I ask you, li'l girl?" Porsche turned and squinted at the eight- year-old.

A winning smile grew on Vari's face.

Smart-mouthed fuckas, Porsche thought, but she didn't say it. She went back to scrolling down her Fa-cebook page. Just about every post in her newsfeed had something to do with Bulletface getting shot at. Photos of his bullet-riddled Bugatti were being shared. Some people were posting worried comments, while others were calling him dumb for even showing his face in Chicago after being threatened at the concert the night before.

There was a lot of speculation as to whether or not he and his MBM artists were in anyway involved in the other Lawndale shootings.

"Bulletface got the Book turnt up!" Porsche said, full of excitement as she turned in her chair. Her ex-citement ceased abruptly.

Alexus was standing in the bedroom doorway with a gold-plated M- 16 assault rifle cradled in her hands.

"Everybody get dressed," she said. "We're leaving. King and Vari, you two come with me."

Chapter 14

Blake was already awake and dressed in a black Versace shirt over baggy denim shorts and Louis Vuit-ton sneakers when his son and daughter joined him in his walk-in closet. Alexus was seconds behind them.

"Daddy," King said, "why Momma got a gun? Vari said it's cause Momma's crazy like you."

Alexus laughed and gave King a gentle slap to the back of the head. "Shut your mouth, King."

"Ha-ha," Vari teased.

King glowered at his sister and raised his fist in a threatening gesture; Vari knocked his fist down and went back to playing Scrabble on her smartphone.

"I'll fuck you up," King warned.

Blake chuckled and scooped up his son just as Alexus was moving in for another slap. He shielded it with his forearm. "Get off my li'l homie," he said, ducking and jogging out of her reach.

"Make him apologize." Alexus planted her hands on her hips. A shoulder strap encircling the nape of her neck had her golden assault rifle hanging across her ample cleavage. "Now," she demanded.

Vari mimicked her stepmother's hand-on-hips pose.

"Okay," Blake said, putting King down behind him. "Vari apologize to your brother for teasing him first."

"Are you serious?" Alexus asked incredulously.

Vari sucked her teeth and squinted at Blake as he put on a gold-buckled Louis Vuitton belt. "I didn't tease that boy."

"Yes you did," Blake refuted. "You said 'ha-ha' when she—" he jabbed an accusatory index finger at Alexus – "slapped him."

The girls went silent for a long moment, both casting contemptuous stares at the man of the house. Intent on dragging the little disagreement our for as long as he possibly could, Blake took his time selecting two white diamond necklaces from his jewelry cabinet then added an equally blingy Rolex watch and bracelet to his wrists.

King Neal ended the silent standoff.

"I apologize, big sister," he said, stepping out from behind Blake's legs with a hint of a smile on his face.

Seemingly, content with the apology, Alexus ordered the kids to the bedroom so she and Blake could talk. Apparently, she wasn't as content with the apology as she seemed; she slapped King hard across the back of the head as he ran past. He hit the ground and hopped up laughing.

"Your son is just as fucked up in the head as you are," Alexus said, still holding her hips.

Blake moved in quickly, lifting the strap from around his wife's neck, and leaning the M-16 against the wall as he applied a gentle kiss to her lips. He moved his hands to her ass and squeezed.

"You check out your new iPhone?" she asked.

He shook his head no. "Got it in my back pocket."

"Apple doesn't want them seen in public until they're released next month, so make sure you keep it put up."

"Why you got the choppa out in front of the kids?"

Alexus sighed and rested the side of her face on Blake's shoulder, softly raking her fingernails across his neck. "Some guys claiming to be ISIS have a hit on me. Sneed called and said they're planning to attack me sometime today."

"Don't worry about that shit, baby."

"I'm not. Enrique called in fifty-six more armed men to beef up our security and make sure my mom is safe across the street. Plus, Sneed has a team of FBI agents down—"

"Stop talkin' to that muhfucka!"

"He's not a threat. I've got enough dirt on him to crush any case he tries to bring against me."

"So what? He's still the Feds."

"Oh, shut up. I got this." She pressed her lips to the side of his neck and let the kiss linger, then pulled back and studied his eyes with a guilty smirk on her face. "I need to ask you something," she said soft-ly."Nope," he hastily replied. "Let me ask first, damn." "Go ahead."

"Well," she said, her smirk expanding, "since you decided to have a bachelor party last night, it seems only right that I have some fun, too."

Blake was already shaking his head. "Nuh-uh. Not unless you gon' have all female dancers."

"Now you know that's not fair," Alexus countered.

"Life ain't fair," Blake reasoned, cupping her think derriere and grinning broadly. "We're married; the only dick you gon' have swingin' in yo' face is mine. And don't forget that I didn't plan that party."

"Neither will I."

"Nope. Not gonna happen."

"Ugh, I fucking hate you. Black-ass." She crossed her arms and pouted, gazing into his eyes in an obvi-ous attempt at changing his mind.

It didn't work. There was no way he was going to let his two-month- pregnant wife turn up with a bunch of semi-naked men.

Alexus showed a sudden smile, and Blake knew she was getting ready to make another chess move.

She put the palms of her hands on his chest and shoved him into the spacious bathroom they shared be-tween their gaudily accessorized walk-in closets. Stumbling rearward, he watched her shut and lock the door. Then she sashayed across the white marble floor to the door leading in from her own closet and did the same to it.

"Don't push me again," Blake threatened with a refulgent diamond grin.

Slowly, one foot in front of the other like a runway model, Alexus walked to him.

"Nah, I ain't goin'. I ain't goin' at gunpoint." Blake's grin grew rapidly. He sat on the smooth marble edge of the Jacuzzi and chuckled at her lustful expression. "You think you can get me like this all the time?"

"Like what?" She kneeled between his parted legs and began unbuckling his belt with her right hand while she bit down on her other thumbnail. She opened his jeans dug in the hole of his boxers, and tugged out his heavy black phallus.

She immediately sucked the large head of it into her mouth and held it there, squeezing, and stroking its length until it because as rigid as a flagpole in her hands. The she popped it out of her mouth and smiled up at him. "If you like feeling this, I'd advise you to let me get my way," she said.

"Don't play wit' me, Alexus." "I'm dead-ass serious."

Blake didn't feel like arguing – not with his dick standing so tall and erect. Maybe allowing his wife to attend her own little stripper party would have her hot and horny when she made it home to him.

Damn, he thought. She checkmated me.

Alexus seemed to read the resolve in his eyes. She pulled his jeans and boxers down to his knees and made the majority of his twelve thick inches vanish into her throat.

Just then, Blake's iPhone 5 rang in his front right pocket.

Alexus dug in the pocket and glanced at the smartphone's screen before handing it to Blake, all the while keeping his length buried in her throat. She began sucking his dick in and out of her mouth as soon as he answered the call.

It was Meach.

"What up, bruh?" Blake answered.

"Nigga, what the fuck happened after we split up last night? Who shot the Bugatti up?"

"Wish I knew. I'll talk to you about it." Blake was reluctant to converse about crimes over the phone. Though he knew signal scramblers were implanted in every phone in his wife's circle, he was still leery of wiretaps.

"On Angelo," Meach said, "you should've come to our room, bruh. All the strippers in here wit' us right now. Maliah went nuts pussy poppin'

and bouncin' that fat ass. I threw 'bout twenty racks at her and Nona."

"They still there?"

"Hell yeah. We just ate breakfast. In a smoke session, right now.

You gotta see Maliah in these jeans she got on. Ass so fat I need a lap dance, on Lo. You need to bring yo' ass down here. We got the whole fortieth floor."

"Give me about twenty minutes."

"Awready. Solid world," Meach said, and ended the call.

Alexus's mouth was like a jackhammer on Blake's dick. The diamond-encrusted double-C Chanel ear-rings she wore were swinging rapidly. Her saliva was sliding down his glistening black pole. He leaned back and watched her work her oral magic, loving the feel of her tightly sucking mouth.

Checking his phone, he saw that he had two new text messages from his music manager concerning that night's concert at the Georgia Dome in Atlanta. There were numerous messages from worried music industry moguls and recording artists. His uncle, Noble, was also worried, as well as his friends and distant relatives.

He put down the smartphone and focused on his beautiful wife's sexy green eyes as she fellated him with ease. Sliding her lips up to the head, she streaked his long muscle and sucked harder.

In seconds, his hips were straining forward, his chest was heaving, and then in a tense moment of re-lease, he erupted in three long, draining spurts. Sticky white semen trickled from the corners of his wife's mouth. He let out a heavy breath and chuckled.

She gulped down his goo, licked up the remaining cum that had escaped her tight oral grip, and stood up smiling.

"You liked that, didn't you?" she asked, and leaned toward him for a kiss.

He pushed her face away. "Don't fuck around and get Chris Browned," he said, pulling up his boxers and jeans. "You can go ahead and have that party, but I swear to God, if you do anything to piss me off—"

"I won't," she chirped."I'll Ray Rice yo' muhfuckin' ass."

"You ain't gon' do shit."

"Yeah, a'ight. Find out the hard way."

Alexus rolled her eyes. "I'm taking the kids to Six Flags for the day. Do you plan on staying in Atlanta tonight or are you coming home? Oh, and while you're getting on me about my bachelorette party, you," she jabbed her index fingernail into his shirt, "better keep your damned hands to yourself at that show."

"I'll be home tonight." He grinned, already contemplating blowing $100,000 or so at a strip club after the concert. "Don't do that," Alexus said.

"Do what?"

"That grin. You're up to something." "I ain't allowed to smile now?"

She squinted at him. Her hands went to her hips. "Okay baby. I'll be good. Promise," Blake said.

After gargling some mouthwash, Alexus preceded Blake to their bedroom. He hugged the kids goodbye and walked them to the front door. Mercedes was standing there with Enrique and a dozen more body-guards.

"Porsche just left out with Biggs," Mercedes said without looking up from her smartphone. She was a certified dime piece in her snug black dress and matching Louboutin heels.

Blake hugged Alexus and gave her a kiss on the cheek. "I'ma hit the studio wit' the gang before we head to the airport. I'll call you before takeoff."

"Be safe," she said.

Blake watched them leave, and ten minutes later, he too vacated the penthouse, completely unaware of the dangers that awaited him and his family.

Chapter 15

Usually there were four armed bodyguards waiting on Blake when he left out every morning; that morn-ing there was twelve.

Two of them carried his twin Louis Vuitton duffle bags, while two others wheeled along behind them with his two matching suitcases. On the elevator, he called his music manager, got no answer, and decided not to phone anyone else. At least not then. He had to ruminate over the war he was knee deep in. The night before could have easily been his last night, and though he was more than ready for war, he was not willing to give up his life or freedom in the process of battling his enemies.

A FaceTime call from Alexus shook him from his thoughts just as the elevator door opened onto the fortieth floor. He was surprised to see Porsche and Biggs standing with Meach and Scrill near the open door of the first room to his left.

Alexus said, "Just letting you know that we made it safely into the van." She laughed nervously. "I wish Sneed wouldn't have told me about that threat. Now I can't stop looking over my shoulder."

"Told you not to worry about that shit," Blake said.

"Did you eat breakfast? I left you a plate in the microwave." "I ate it."

"You need to eat me." She beamed.

"Soon's I get home tonight." "Promise?"

"Of course."

"Vari said you forgot to get her a pizza yesterday."

"Well, make that right for me. I gotta go, baby. I'll call you back.

Love you," he said.

"Love you."

He dropped the phone in his pocket and shook hands with Biggs first. After they'd shot up the minivan, Biggs had taken the guns and ditched them in a garage on Troy Street. He'd been right on time. The cops had pulled Blake over before Biggs made it back to the Bugatti.

Young Meach had a bandage on his left wrist, and his right arm was in a sling. A few days earlier, a bullet had pounded through his shoulder and another had grazed his wrist during a shootout in Gary. He only wore the sling when the shoulder wound ached. He and Scrill were dressed like Blake in Versace and Louis Vuitton with big white diamonds in their jewelry, and both of them were sipping from gold bottles of Ace of Spades.

"Shit got heavy last night, didn't it?" Meach asked. "Fucked my arm up lettin' that K blow. I tried talkin' to the li'l niggas in that Excursion, but shorty in the backseat upped strap on me."

"Got his whole ball cap pushed back," Will Scrill added. "Fuck niggas hopped out on us at the red light," Blake said. He nudged an elbow into Biggs' shoulder. "Bruh got down wit' me. Glad I had that muhfucka bulletproofed."

"You ain't the only one glad," Biggs said.

There was a rolled blunt resting behind Meach's ear. Blake took it and put fire to its end. He smoked and discussed the threat ISIS posed to his wife, trying his best to ignore Porsche's blatant stare as she stood next to him with her hands on her hips.

The conversation trailed off as the door across the hall from them opened. Nona stepped out first, wear-ing a small pink mini-dress and heels. Then came Blacc Chyna in a black YMCMB shirt over black leggings and heels, and finally, Maliah in a small white t-shirt over low-cut blue jeans that showed off her incredibly meaty derriere. A Kevin Gates song was playing in their room. Each of the three woman had their own gold bottle of champagne, and the eyes of their beautiful reddish-brown faces were glued to Blake.

"Hey, Mr. Bulletface," Maliah said. She walked over and hugged him. "I was seriously hoping I'd get to see you again before my flight back to Houston. We really didn't get a chance to talk."

"We sure didn't," Chyna said, and hugged his other side.

Grinning and shaking his head, Blake fought to come up with an easy way to get himself out of the hot water he'd just dived into. Flanking him was two of the baddest redbones he'd ever laid eyes on, but he was now a married man. His wife was two months pregnant. As bad as he wanted to talk to Chyna and Ma-liah, he knew he couldn't do it.

They all headed into Meach's presidential suite. In an effort to keep his mind off the dime piece strippers, he dug his diamond-encrusted Beats headphones out of a suitcase, plugged them into his smartphone, and listened to a beat Mannie Fresh and emailed him a few days earlier. He sat between Biggs and Meach on the soft leather sofa, nodding his head to the beat as the guys began rolling blunts and filling their Styrofoam cups with ice, Sprite, and Promethazine with Codeine.

Maliah was persistent.

She crossed the room to Blake and pushed the headphones off his ears. "You need to lock my number in your phone in case you and Alexus ever call it quits. One of these days I am going to have my way with you, and when I do..." She bit down on her bottom lip.

Her sexy expression made Blake's dick swell in his pants. His iPhone 6 rang, and then all hell broke loose.

King Rio

Chapter 16

31...32...33...

Jose Ramirez stared at the glowing numbers as the elevator continued its rapid climb up the Trump Tow-er. His heart was pounding. His adrenal glands were on fire. The single-button remote taped to his right wrist was connected to the C-4 explosives that were wrapped around the vest he wore beneath his suit jacket.

34...35...

The Feds were onto him. He was certain of it. He'd seen them watching him when he parked his yellow BMW in front of the building, and he figured at least one of them was observing him from the camera in the corner of the ceiling behind him, but neither obstacle mattered. They were too late. He and the four other men who'd been entrusted with the task of killing Alexus Costilla and her family were too close to their target to fail now.

38...39...40

Ding!

He snapped open his briefcase, retrieved the Uzi submachine gun from inside it, and let the briefcase clatter to the floor as the door began to open.

There were two bodyguards standing outside a door on the hallway's left side. Jose pulled the trigger as he rushed toward them. One round punched a hole in the first bodyguard's neck, and as he reached for the wound, two more plowed through the flesh below his right eye. He collapsed against the wall a half-second after his brain did.

The dead man's partner dove to the floor, drawing a pistol from his hip and taking aim at Jose as Jose took aim at him. Jose's rapid fire caught the bodyguard first, etching holes into the chest of his black Hartmarx suit jacket. A bullet whizzed past Jose's left ear.

Instinctively, Jose flung an index finger to the button on his wrist.

King Rio

Chapter 17

"I've got a bad feeling in the pit of my stomach, Enrique, and it's not morning sickness," Alexus said.

She twisted and turned her white diamond tennis bracelet around her wrist, a nervous habit of hers. She looked to her left. Mercedes was sitting there, gazing thoughtfully out the Sprinter's large side window as the big white van zipped up Lake Shore Drive. It was one of Alexus's favorite views; the vast, rippling blue waters of Lake Michigan, its skyline replete with skyscrapers and brilliant rays of sun. They had just stopped at Dominos for pizza; Savaria and King Neal were chowing down in their seats behind Alexus, and Enrique, seated across from her, was biting into a hot wing.

In Spanish, (because he knew that neither Mercedes, Vari, nor King would understand him), Enrique said, "No worries, Lexi. I've protected you this long, have I not? I kept your grandmother safe, too, through dozens of wars with the Los Zetas and Sinaloas, numerous assassination attempts."

You name it, I've been through it, and I know how to handle it. You can relax. Here, have a bite."

He offered his box of hot wings, but she declined. She had three of her own boxes of hot wings stacked next to the laptop computer on the table in front of her.

Although Alexus had already devoured a three-course breakfast barely two hours earlier, she found her-self suddenly ravenous. She seemed to gobble down the first box in just a few bites, and she was tearing into the second box when Enrique's smartphone rang.

He answered, and his eyes grew wide. He swallowed a mouthful of scrumptious chicken and said, in Spanish, "There's been a bombing at the Trump!"

Alexus gasped in horror.

"What the hell did he just say?" Mercedes said worriedly. Suddenly, the van came to a screeching halt in the middle of Lake Shore Drive. The two identical Sprinters driving ahead of it also stopped.

"Oh, shit!" Mercedes pointed at her window.

Enrique and Alexus moved to the window and peered out.

There were two small cars parked head-to-head, blocking off traffic.

A man with a black scarf wrapped around his head was down on one knee with a shoulder-mounted rocket launcher aimed at the trio of Mercedes vans.

"Pull back!" Enrique shouted just as a rocket came soaring in their direction.

The van directly in front of them bounced into the sky atop a plume of flames.

Chapter 18

Blake's security team had rushed to the door at the sound of gunfire, snatching submachine guns from inside their crisp black blazers and urging everyone else to retreat to the suite's second level.

Meach always kept guns laying on the ottomans in his hotel rooms. Blake had grabbed one of them (a .45 caliber Glock with an extended clip) before turning and hurriedly ushering the panic-stricken strippers up the staircase.

Then a massive, deafening explosion had rocked the luxury suite, immediately filling the room with smoke and flying debris. The front wall and the door disintegrated into fiery rubble. The sheer force of the blast knocked everyone down, and Blake landed on Nona's back just as the smoke alarm and sprinklers went off.

Through ringing ears, he heard himself ask her if she was okay. He turned over onto his butt on the top step and sat there, stunned.

His instincts kicked in.

He ran back down the stairs and hurried over to where his suitcases and duffle bags had been left near the sofa. His fingers trembled as he pulled on the zipper of a suitcase, but he managed to open it in a matter of seconds.

Inside the big leather suitcase was five million in bank-new Benjamin Franklins, separated into ten-thousand dollar packets; a smaller version of the Kalashnikov AK-47; and a 200-round drum magazine.

He attached the drum to the assault rifle.

"Goddamn," Porsche said as she scrambled to his side. "That was a bomb, wasn't it?"

"Get me the fuck out of here!" Nona cried wobbling on her heels as her brother helped her down the stairs.

Five bodyguards struggled to their feet, two of them seriously injured. The others lay unmoving on the bloodied floor, their bodies twisted disproportionately and mangle beyond recognition.

The sprinklers weakened the flames. Meach and Scrill did all they could to calm the girls down while the three dazed bodyguards moved out into the charred hallway with their guns drawn. They gave the all clear a moment later, and the girls rant to their suite to gather their things.

Blake had Biggs grab the duffels. The two injured bodyguards were able to lug the suitcases into the hallway. Leading the way with his AK-47 in hand, coughing his way through the heavy black smoke, Blake entered the hallway, saw that the elevator had not survived the blast, and headed to the stairwell at the other end of the hall.

The door was open, and his uninjured bodyguards were already securing the stairwell in military for-mation.

Porsche hugged him. "Please keep me safe," she said, and hugged him tighter.

With the others in line behind him, Blake started down the stairs. Dozens of frightened Trump guests were spilling into the stairwell, in a frantic haste to make it out of the hotel and live another day.

Blake remained vigilant. His keen brown eyes darted in every direction, inspecting every face.

He was just passing the door on the thirty-seventh floor when one particular expression captured his attention. It was the face of a slender Hispanic man in a cheap-looking pinstriped business suit. He shot a very brief glance at Blake as he entered the stairwell from the thirty-sixth floor. Blake squinted at him and raised the AK. He heard Porsche gasp next to him.

The man's left hand swung over to his right wrist. "Death to America!" he shouted.

Acting on instinct, Blake quickly took aim at the man's head and pulled the trigger. A rapid three-round burst glued half of his head to the wall, and the bodyguards followed up with what sound like twenty more loud gunshots.

The people screamed and ran faster, and everyone made it safely to the ground floor.

Chapter 19

Alexus listened to the sharp crack of gunfire as her driver sped off in revers; the bodyguards in the lead van had just leapt out with their FN-P90 submachine guns ablaze.

"Oh, my God," Alexus murmured, still staring at the scarf-headed terrorist as her security team's bullets riddled his body.

She witnessed a second scarfed head rise up from between the two cars that were blocking the road.

The second terrorist also had a rocket launcher on his shoulder.

Suddenly, the magnificent views of Lake Shore Drive didn't seem so appealing to Alexus.

She hurried to her seat and engaged the seatbelt. "What was that, Ma?" Vari asked, already crying. "Just stay in your seatbelt," Alexus said.

Squeezing her eyes shut, she mumbled a prayer for safety and braced herself for the rocket's impact.

It never came.

A sliver Buick sedan that had been reversing in an attempt to escape the brazen terrorist attack fell victim to the perilous rocket, exploding into the sky mere inches to the left of the Sprinter van.

Alexus held her breath and prayed some more. She opened her eyes and looked at her sister's window just as the Buick came crashing to the ground.

The van whipped around on screeching tires and took off. "You're fired!" Alexus shouted at Enrique.

"Settle down. I'm on it." He dialed a number on his smartphone.

"What do you mean you're on it? Those guys could have blown us to the moon!"

"Well, they didn't. Not yet, anyway. Losing your wits about it won't solve a thing."

"You're fired!"

"You said that already."

Vexed, Alexus gritted her teeth together, forcing herself to be angry with Enrique instead of breaking down in a fit of tears.

King Neal unlatched himself from his car seat and ran to his mother. Climbing onto her lap and curling his little arms tightly around her neck, he said, "I want my daddy," and then started crying.

She cried too, rubbing his back with one hand, clenching her armrest with the other.

More gunshots boomed in the distance. Then came another explosion.

Alexus squeezed her son tight against her bosom and waited for the nightmare to end.

Chapter 20

"You captured the hearts of women all across America with the bestselling "Side Chic" series last year. Now it's being made into a major motion picture by Lionsgate Films?"

La'Tonya West nodded her head, smiling modestly. The beautiful brown-skinned woman was the first guest on "The Rita Bishop Show." She donned a stunning white Versace gown that accentuated her gener-ous curves.

"Yes," she said, giving another nod as the diverse Harpo Studios audience applauded her success. "Sa-naa Latham is cast as LaLa, the main character. I'm still overwhelmed by that. She's always been one of my favorite actresses. Tyson Beckford – another one of my favorites – will be playing her love interest. The film is due to be released next summer."

"Tyson Beckford." Rita turned to the audience wearing a suggestive smirk. "How about that ladies?"

More applause.

La'Tonya blushed, smirked, and shook her head as a shirtless photo of Mr. Beckford appeared on the massive television monitor at the rear of the stage.

"How did a small-town Virginia girl like yourself become such an amazing author? Who are some of your influences?"

"I've pretty much always been a fan of urban books. K'wan, Wahida Clark, Nikki Turner, Keisha Ervin; I liked their books, and if there's one thing I didn't like, it was working for someone else. I wanted to be my own boss, to spend more time with my kids, so I tried my hand at writing."

"Well, you did a wonderful job." "Thank you."

"I mean it. I've read the entire series, and I cannot wait for the movie." Rita looked into the camera. "To-day you're all going home with the "Side Chic" series. Stay tuned. Coming up next is the star of "Side Chic" herself, Ms. Sanaa Latham, followed by a performance from Grammy- award-winning singer Jennifer Hudson."

Rita learned of the terrorist attacks during the commercial break, and by the grace of God, she was able to keep her composure until the show wrapped up forty minutes later.

Tears grew in her eyes the instant she and Attorney Bostic were alone in the backseat of her sleek black Rolls Royce.

"Sounds like that island might not've been such a bad idea," Britney said matter-of-factly. "I spoke with Alexus before they made it to the airport. She said she's gonna call you as soon as her flight lands in Mexico."

"She heading to Matamoras?"

"No." Britney hesitated; then, "She's going down to Juarez City to meet with the cartel's underbosses."

"With my grandson?"

"She's not that crazy. They're at the therapist's office with Tamera and Melz. She wants you to take them to the Palm Island mansion in Miami. Blake's still gonna do his show in Atlanta tonight; he'll be flying in to Miami, too. Alexus will meet us there in the morning."

Swiping away the tears with the tips of her thumbnails, Rita shook her head. "I'm taking them to the island," she said, and went to the CNN app on her smartphone just as her driver pulled the Phantom away from the curb, followed by three equally armored black Escalades, and led by a CPD patrol car.

Rita perused the article describing the attacks:

ISIS Targets American Billionaire Couple

The Islamic State has released a statement on Twitter claiming responsibility for the deadly assassina-tion attempts on Costilla Corp. CEO Alexus Costilla and rapper Bulletface, both of whom reportedly survived the attacks, which claimed the lives of 21 individuals, including the four alleged suspects.

Blake "Bulletface" King is being hailed as a hero by numerous eyewitnesses who report seeing him shoot one suspect in the stairwell at Chicago's Trump International Hotel and Tower...Rita's heart was knocking at her ribcage like a determined Jehovah's Witness. She turned to her window and stared out at the passing buildings, then yanked her Chanel-clothed curtains shut just as a swarm of pitch black Suburbans and Hummers fell in line behind and ahead of her motorcade.

"That's the FBI," Britney explained. "This is ridiculous," Rita said.

"It's necessary. The most dangerous terrorist organization in the world is after your daughter, and they're no longer just a threat to the Middle East. They are right here in America. Sneed believes up to eighty percent of the MS-13 gang has converted to the Islamic State. Congress just voted to begin airstrikes on that new branch of ISIS in Central America, and raids are being conducted on over two hundred homes from Califor-nia to New York as we speak. The Mexican military is also gearing up for the imminent war against these terrorists. We need to be just as ready." Britney opened her big white leather Chanel shoulder bag and took out her iPhone. "Blake's waiting on us at Dr. Farr's office. We'll go to the airport together.

Let him talk to the little ones about what's going on before he leaves." "He shouldn't be leaving in the first place."

"Relax. Everything's fine."

"Everything's fine? Really? We're being escorted through Chicago by the FBI. Things aren't fine."

Frustrated and nearly frightened, Rita decided to call her boyfriend, ex-homicide detective Neal Miller. The ear-pleasing sound of his deep, gruff voice never failed to soothe her soul. She stayed on the line with him all the way to Dr. Farr's office.

King Rio

Chapter 21

A fleet of matte black foreign cars – four Rolls Royces, four Maybach Landaulets, a Ferrari, and a Lam-borghini – surrounded Blake's long black Bulletface tour bus, crowding North Rush Street in front of Dr. Melonie Farr's office building. Three Sprinter vans were strategically parked further up the street, clear signs of Costilla Cartel security.

There was a compact recording booth in the front of the tour bus.

Blake was sitting on the L-shaped black leather sofa directly across from it with King Neal on one knee and Savaria on the other listening to them describe their contradicting versions of what had happened on Lake Shore Drive.

"And the bomb came down the sky," King said, raising his fist above his head for emphasis, "and boom, it blowed the car way up to the stars and the moon."

"A bomb didn't fall from the sky, King. The man had a big gun that shoot that kind of bomb," Vari ar-gued.

"No he didn't."

"He did."

"Nuh-uh."

Vari rolled her eyes. "Whatever you say, airhead."

"I'm not no airhead," King replied, scowling with discontent.

Blake laughed. After a quick shower to cleanse the dark soot of the smoke from his skin, he'd changed into an all-white Louis Vuitton outfit with a matching, left-leaning skullcap. Even the bulletproof vest he wore beneath his shirt was covered in LV logos. He'd given Biggs (who was sitting between Nona and Meach at the other end of the sofa) a similar outfit, along with a rose gold and diamond Rolex watch, a duffle bag containing $500,000 in hundreds, a Mac-11 submachine gun with a 50- round clip, and the Maybach convertible that was parked behind the bus.

Porsche was resting in Blake's bed in the back.

Blake looked up as Dr. Farr entered the side door with his mother- in-law. The kids abandoned his lap and ran over to hug their grandma.""I got some words for you," Rita said to Blake. "What are you doing leaving for a show at a time like this? You should be with these babies, you and Alexus both."

"I can't cancel a Georgia Dome concert at the last minute. I'll be home with them right after the concert, and I'm canceling the show I've got tomorrow."

"Need to cancel the one you got today." Rita dug in her purse and gave Vari and King each a piece of chewing gum.

"Can't do that," Blake said. "My fans gotta see me on that stage tonight. I done had two separate inci-dents where I could've died in the last twelve hours. Gotta let the streets know I'm good, just one time. I'll cut the rest of the tour and make up for those dates when everything calms down."

Rita regarded him with a tight stare.

The tour bus lurched away from the curb as its driver began the journey to O'Hare International Airport. Rita and the kids headed into Blake's bedroom and shut the door. It was then that Blake realized he'd been holding his breath, anticipating an intense scolding from his wife's mother. She should have known better. Rita never got angry.

"Damn," Biggs said. "I see where Alexus got all dat ass from." "On Angelo," Meach agreed. "I'll fuck the shit out her old ass. Bet she a freak, too."

Dr. Farr shook her head and sauntered off to join Rita and the kids, and Nona rolled her eyes.

"Nasty ass niggas," Nona said, sneering at Blake. She was still pissed at him for leaving her for Alexus, he knew it, but he didn't care. Alexus was his everything. Nothing could change that.

He looked out his window, half-expecting to see a missile flying his way. His smartphones were ringing off the hook, but he only wanted to talk to his wife, and since none of the calls were from her, he ignored them.

He'd only had a couple of seconds to talk to Alexus before she boarded her private jet.

"I'm fine, the kids are fine – everything's good," she'd said. "Pick King and Vari up from Melonie's office. I'm taking a quick trip to Mexico,

be right back in the morning. Take my mom and kids to the airport so they can get away from this mad-ness in Chicago. Go ahead to your Atlanta show. Just meet me in Miami afterwards. We can spend some alone time at the Versace Mansion, break in a few more rooms. Maybe the studio."

Blake had grinned suggestively, muttered, "Love you," and then Alexus had ended the FaceTime call.

Now he envisioned himself fucking her in the recording studio, and he couldn't wait to make it a reality.

King Rio

Chapter 22

'Soon's I leave da trap I hit da club, my pockets swole like Rambo
Pull up in that Lambo wit' that chop-pa on me like Rambo
All da bad bitches can stay wit' me but you fuck-niggas better scram, though
'Cause y'all gossip like Wendy Williams and I end the shit like Rambo Dub Life what I am, hoe
Young Bulletface I'm the man, though The nigga no nigga gon' stand on Big strap I'ma keep my hand on
And I swear da clip so damn long Forty-five wit' extendo
Make yo' niggas duck when my niggas hunt And bitch we ain't playin' Nintendo Choppa on me, I'm Rambo
Choppa on me, I'm Rambo Made dirty money off grams, hoe
Middle fingas up to Uncle Sambo
My hittas strapped, wearin' all black From MC to Chiraq, nigga
Hoes love how shiny this ice is
And we terrorists to these rat niggas I'm laid back in my Maybach
Bumpin' Young Meach, dat straight crack
Bad bitch next to me suck me up Then clean it up like Ajax...'
Blake was in full Bulletface mode. Holding a double Styrofoam of Lean in one hand and an obese cigarillo of Kush between the thumb and forefinger of his other, Blake was standing at the mic in the recording booth inside fellow rapper T.I.'s Atlanta home, freestyling a verse to "Rambo," a song that would be released on his upcoming "Took the Throne" album.

The track featured epic verses from T.I., Lil Wayne, and Jeezy; the trio of expert southern lyricists was peering in through the booth's soundproof glass, nodding their heads to the music. Like Blake's, their entourages were already enroute to the Georgia Dome for the night's Bulletface concert.

Biggs and Nona had parted ways with Blake four hours earlier at the airport in Chicago. Porsche had decided against joining Rita and the kids on their flight to Rita's private tropical island. Choosing instead to stick by Blake's side all the way to Atlanta, sleeping next to him on his Gulfstream 650, sauntering alongside him through the Atlanta airport and accompanying him and his MBM artists to his thirty-million dollar Atlanta mansion. He and Alexus had only been there twice since he purchase it during their honeymoon in Ibiza, but Alexus already had the place fully furnished with his and hers Ferraris in the garage.

Porsche had been in the passenger seat of his Ferrari during the brief drive to Tip's place, and now she was in the far right corner of the studio with her eyes glued to him as he rapped.

His iPhone 6 rang as he stepped out of the booth, a FaceTime video call from Alexus.

As soon as her flawless visage appeared on the screen, Blake smiled. Alexus smiled back.

"I miss you already," she said, and blew him a kiss.

Then a flash of fully automatic gunfire illuminated the space behind her.

Chapter 23

"What the fuck was that?" Blake asked. The gunfire continued.

Alexus turned the camera so that Blake could see the long line of Mexican men that were being gunned down in the middle of a deserted stretch of road in Mexico City, Mexico.

Their hands were cuffed behind their backs, and their heads were jerking forward as the Mexican Mili-tary soldiers and Costilla Cartel militants behind them used AK-47s to shoot the brains from their skulls.

A motorcade of armored Hummers and military tanks packed the dusty serpentine road from end to end. Twelve Apache attack helicopters hovered high up in the sky, overhead eyes for Alexus, and the three thousand soldiers she had on the ground with her.

She was standing next to her snow-white Rolls Royce Phantom, a chilled bottle of water in one hand, her iPhone 6 in the other. Mouth and eyes agape, Mercedes Costilla stood to the left of Alexus, gawking in horror at the brazen executions.

Their uncle Flako Costilla and his son Pedro were overseeing the beheadings of their slaughtered hostag-es, and Enrique was standing to the right of Alexus, as silent as a church mouse and ever watchful.

"We caught these guys before they could get to our Matamoras home," Alexus said, turning the smartphone's front camera back to her face. "There's a hundred and forty-seven of them here, all members of that new branch of ISIS. Twenty of them were high-ranking. I'm sending their heads back to their homes, leave them burning on their front steps. Seven thousand Mexican soldiers are already on the way to destroy their strongholds in Central America, and U.S. air forces are flying reconnaissance missions over those regions as we speak. Bombings should be starting any minute."

"You're turning into a female version of Papi," Blake said with a half grin.

"Enrique said that when I ordered the beheadings." She shrugged indifferently as the final gunshot sounded. "These guys deserve it. They were planning to kill me. You know I can't go for that."

"Just to be safe, baby." "Don't worry about me."

"You gon' make me come through there and fuck some shit up." He raised a 30-round clip to his camera and dangled it for her to see. "Make 'em feel these. You know I will."

"Bringing a handgun to Mexico is like bringing a knife to a gunfight. I got this. You just focus on your concert, and figure out something we can do together in the morning. We'll spend at least half the day in Miami, just the two of us."

Alexus attempted an uneasy smile, but then a severed head tumbled to a stop next to her right foot, and the smile vanished. She sucked in a startled breath.

"What's wrong baby?" Blake asked.

"Nothing." She sighed and shook her head. "Take care of yourself in Atlanta. And try not to get shot again, will you? I can't take any more bad news, not today. I'll call you when we get to Matamoras. Love you."

Blake blew her a kiss and ended the call.

Just then, a distant thunder of machine gun fire echoed through the air. Alexus flicked her eyes to En-rique as Mercedes slapped a hand onto her shoulder and murmured, "Get me out of here. Right damned now."

Enrique listened to the speaker in his ear; Uncle Flako and Pedro ceased their beheadings mid-swing and stood frozen in place with blood dripping from the blades of their perilous hatchets.

"It's another ISIS attack," Enrique said.

Seconds later, a helicopter descended to pick them up, and soon they were soaring away from the chaos.

Alexus shut her eyes, dropped her head back, and tried to think of what to do next. She knew that she was safe with the Mexican military on her side. She already had a shipment of 500 million dollars in dirty money on the way for the war, and she was willing to invest a lot more if need be.

A dozen fighter jets roared by overhead. Mercedes shivered next to Alexus. "We are in way over our heads," Mercedes said.

"Girl, I am so scared. I have never seen anything like this in Chicago."

"Shut your scary ass up." Alexus laughed. She too was scared, but she wasn't about to admit it. Not at that moment. She had to be strong for the family. She only allowed herself to let down her security walls when Blake was around. "Don't worry about anything. We're more than ready for whatever we encounter. Just calm down. Let me think."

"I can't calm down. I just watched about a thousand men get their damn heads cut off. You calm down. I don't know why you ordered them to do that in first place. Enrique, you're just as crazy as she is. Get me back to Chicago immediately. I mean right now. And give me some money. At least a million. I want to go somewhere, relax, and get the fuck away from all this shit."

"Relax." Alexus picked up her crocodile skin Birkin bag and pulled out a blunt. It was Kush. The best of the best. She lit it and attempted to pass it to her sister. "Here, bitch. Take a hit of this loud and calm down. I have to think and I can't think with you rattling off all in my ear.

Enrique, make sure that money gets to the military base on time."

Mercedes pushed the blunt away and rolled her eyes. She was obviously frustrated with all that was go-ing on, and Alexus felt responsible. After all, it had been her who ordered the murder of Mercedes and Porsche's mother (though unintentionally), and she knew that had she been a little tighter on family security, Mercedes would not have lost her children to their now deceased aunt Jenny. She'd given Mercedes tons of money since they had first met, but Alexus knew that no amount of money could take the place of a mother. It sure helped, though.

"I think we should all go and stay on the island for a while. At least for a few months." Alexus became thoughtful. She stared at the smoke ring curling up into the air from the tip of the blunt.

Uncle Flako and Pedro lit their own cigars, although theirs were full of Cuban tobacco instead of high-grade marijuana. The two of them still had blood on their hands, and the sight of it nearly sickened Alexus. She wished her father were still alive. Papi had been the most ruthless drug cartel boss in history, much more wealthy and brutal than Pablo Escobar could ever have dreamed of being. Papi had lost his life on the same night that Blake and T-Walk had shot each other in the alley behind a nightclub in Northwest Indiana. Only a few people knew who had fired the fatal shot; Flako and Pedro were among the uninformed.

"What's the point of cutting their heads off? Please tell me that. I can't understand it," Mercedes said.

"Maybe it's not for you to understand." Flako accepted a wet wipe from Alexus and cleaned the blood from his fingertips with it. "You know something? You ain't so tough when you're not in Chicago. I don't think you're built for Mexico." He gave Mercedes a tight-eyed stare.

She scowled and offered him a middle finger. It was funny seeing the way she and her uncle interacted. At least to Alexus it was.

When they made it to the airport, they all boarded the Gulf Stream 6 private jet that Alexus had purchased just two years prior. She took a seat and wished Blake was there with her. Checking her phone, she saw that she had several missed calls from Agent Sneed, and one from her mother. Both would have to wait. It was a time of rumination, a time to ponder over her situation and to make sure that she made the right decision for both herself and her family.

The two flight attendants served crab cakes, shrimp, lobster, 16-ounce steaks, and bottles of Ace of Spades champagne. Mercedes made a special request for vodka; Alexus gulped down half a bottle of champagne before even touching her shrimp. She decided to give Mercedes a little more spending money. $10,000,000 cash. She wouldn't tell her until they made it back to the United States, specifically to Atlanta.

She wanted to get near Blake as soon as possible, not only to make sure he was safe, or to feel safe her-self, but also to watch his sneaky ass.

Blake was a well-known cheater. He had bedded dozens of strippers during their brief separation a few years earlier, and though they were now married, she still wanted to make sure he was being faithful.

"Pop up and surprise his ass," she mumbled to herself as she uploaded a pic to Instagram. She went to Blake's page to look around, being nosey. There were several new pictures of him in the studio at Tip's Atlanta mansion with T.I., Lil Wayne, and Young Jeezy... And Porsche. Porsche was sitting in the corner all by herself, gazing fixedly at Blake.

Alexus didn't like the look.

"Stop drinking so much." Pedro snatched the crystal stem glass from Alexus's hand and set it down on the table in front of her. He was kind of chubby like his father, but he seemed to have lost some weight recently. His finely tailored suit accentuated his corpulent frame. He had a low haircut, all-white suit, and a sparkling pair of Gucci shoes that were also white like the diamonds and his Rolex watch. "You should be on the phone making important calls. Don't turn into a drunk on us. You're the queen of the world now, Lexi. Gotta be able to think clearly in every event."

"This liquor helps me think, Pedro. Smoking and drinking helps me more than you'll ever know. I need an X pill too." She laughed nervously.

Her hands were shaking, and her nerves weren't doing much better. "I'll be fine. Don't worry about me. Go get yourself a plate."

Enrique sat across from her. "The cash will be delivered tonight. 500 million dollars even," he said, gaz-ing at Alexus. "So, where are we headed next? And what's going on with Blake? Has he said anything about his performance tonight at the Georgia Dome? I bet everyone's going to show their faces there, especially with that one rapper in the building. I forget his name. The little one with the dreads."

"Blake's fine. But I don't trust him around Porsche. I think she likes him too much, and this morning when I walked into their bedroom, I heard her saying something about Blake."

"I wouldn't trust the bitch either," Mercedes said as she took the seat next to Alexus. "Remember I told you how I caught her with my man, had to fuck both of them up." She nibbled on a piece of red velvet cake and lifted the curtain on her window. The plane was just taking off.

Alexus shook her head. "She wouldn't do me like that. Well, I hope not. After all I've done for her; she would be a dirty bitch if she fucked me over."

"That's just it. She's a dirty bitch. If she slept with my man and she and I have the same mother, what do you think she's going to do to you when your boyfriend is the most sought-after rapper in the whole world? Don't be naive. You better watch that bitch. I'll never leave her around anything of mine again. I didn't even want her looking at Biggs like that. Did you see how buff that boy was? Blake should have been brought him around. I tell you this much, if I ever get my hands on that nigga, I'm fucking his brains out, and I'm keeping him away from Porsche."

Alexus laughed again, but she was seriously considering what Mercedes was saying. Would Blake actu-ally cheat on her with that little ratchet hood girl? She thought of Janautica, the ratchet North Carolina girl Blake had cheated on her with before, and suddenly Mercedes's suspicions didn't seem so outlandish.

Instinctively, she FaceTimed Blake. An audible sigh of relief blew from her lips when he answered. His picturesque grin filled the screen and warmed her heart. She giggled at herself for thinking she'd bust him cheating.

"What, baby? Damn. I gotta work," he said, rubbing a hand forward across his short crop of wavy hair. He seemed stressed.

"Okay, okay. I'm just worried, Blake. I've never been attacked by ISIS terrorists before."

"I'm good, baby. I'll call you when I get some free time. Too busy right now."

"Keep your hands to yourself, will you?"

"What?" He knitted his brows together quizzically.

"You know what the fuck I mean. Just what I said. Keep your hands to yourself. You know I don't trust you around any bitch. You'll stick your dick right in if she opens her legs."

"Who? What are you talking about?"

"Just do as I say and we won't have any problems. Comprende?" He chuckled, frowned. "Bye, baby."

"I love you, Blake. That's the only reason I'm jealous. You've cheated on me before and I'm afraid it might happen again."

"With who? Ain't nobody here but Porsche and Tiny." "Mm hmm."

"Bye, baby," he repeated, and that time he hung up.

Alexus took a sobering breath and looked over at Mercedes. Though the two of them had different moth-ers, they looked remarkably alike. It was almost eerie. Alexus had gone 19 years without ever having met Mercedes. It was crazy to know that she'd had a near twin who had grown up poor in Chicago while she herself had lived a fairly well off life in southern Texas and northern Mexico. Mercedes had prostituted her body and time to older men to pay the bills for the majority of her teenage life; during the same span of time, Alexus had been dealing kilos of cocaine and learning how to be a cartel boss from their father.

"Like I said, watch that bitch," Mercedes advised. "That's my little sister and I love her to death, but it is what it is. She's a nympho. That girl has literally fucked everybody in our old neighborhood, all up and down Lake Street, all up and down Chicago Avenue, all up and down North Avenue, and even out south. Don't let that sweet face fool you. She'll be sucking your man's dick before you know it."

Alexus looked at Enrique. "Change of plans. We're going to Atlanta."

King Rio

Chapter 24

Lean, OG Kush, and Yo Gotti bumping in Blake's foreign car was all he needed to calm his nerves and ready himself for the night's performance. Porsche was sitting beside him in silence, stalking people's pages on Instagram, and occasionally hitting the blunt as he drove to the Georgia Dome.

He had just spoken to his music manager, and everything was in order for the show.

"You mind making a quick stop before we go to the concert?" Porsche asked.

"For what?"

"My girl got some pills for me. You know I got to turn up at the show tonight. Backstage action!" She smiled broadly, biting her lower lip. "You need to hook me up with somebody since I can't get what I really want."

"I ain't hooking you up with nobody. Sit your little fast ass down somewhere. You don't need no pills. You ain't even old enough to drink yet."

"In some countries you don't even have to be 21 to drink. I think in Paris you can be like 16."

"Well, we ain't in Paris."

"I know. We in Atlanta, the turn up capital of the world!"

Blake chuckled and shook his head. He stopped at a red light and sipped some Lean, wondering what the hell Alexus had called him tripping about. Jeezy was behind him in an all-black Rolls Royce Phantom. There were seven or eight more foreign cars following along behind them, Jeezy's CTE crew, and some BMF members.

A deep drag from the Kush sent Porsche into a coughing fit. Blake took the blunt back and eyed her soft lips for a moment before speeding off through the green light. Maybe this bitch is the reason Alexus trippin', he thought to himself. A part of him was still on edge. The Trump attacks had him feeling uneasy and more alert than ever. Several of his bodyguards were dead, and the others were severely injured. He'd heard of the terrorists the American troops were fighting in Iraq and Syria, but never would he have thought that the fight would be brought to his own doorstep.

Porsche must have read his mind. She got herself together and said, "That explosion at the hotel was crazy, wasn't it? Man, I'm still shaking.

That kind of shit just don't happen in Chicago. I thought I had seen it all, but ain't no such thing as seeing it all with that damn Costilla Cartel in the picture. You know what's crazy? We grew up dirt poor on the westside of Chicago. I don't think I ever even saw $10,000 before I met Alexus. Now I got a Bentley, my own condo, I'm about to open up my beauty salon, and I might even open up a restaurant. That bitch has given me over a quarter million dollars in the past month alone. She just gave me the money for the party too. Ooh, I cannot wait to get that bachelorette party planned. We gon' do some serious turning up, you feel me?"

Blake gave her an are-you-serious look and kept smoking. He went back to looking out his window, studying his surroundings, and searching for any signs of danger. After all the drama he had gone through over the past few years, he knew he couldn't afford to slip. One slip might mean an eternal fall. He'd come too close to dying, too many times to count already, and the thought of being shot again kept him on high alert. He had a Mac-11 submachine gun on his lap, and attached to it was a red laser beam and an extended 50-round clip. There was also a Glock on his hip with the 30- round clip, and he had an AK-47 in the trunk with a 100-round drum that he was just dying to empty at a fuck-nigga if one so happened to try him. He was dead set on living until the ripe old age of 70 or 80; going out like Tupac or Biggie was not his idea of a good life.

"So, what's up with you and that girl Nona? Y'all fuckin' again?" Porsche was always too nosey for comfort. She took a swallow of water, cleared her throat, and pulled down the visor to check herself out in the mirror. "I can tell she still likes you. Them other bitches wanna give you some pussy too. Don't act like you didn't notice the way they was looking at you. Hell, a blind man could have saw that."

"You need to learn how to mind your own goddamn business."

"You gon' hook me up wit' somebody? Please? I know you got his number."

"These niggas got hoes in every area code. Ain't nobody tryna make you their girlfriend in this industry. You need to find yourself a doctor or lawyer, shit, maybe even a football player. Anybody but a rapper or singer.

Niggas got too many groupies. I don't want no parts of you getting your heart broken. Mercedes ain't about to be blaming me for that shit."

"Pleeeeeeease?"

"Leave me alone, Porsche. Sit back and chill. We almost there." He eased forward in his seat and paid close attention as they passed Morehouse and Spelman colleges.

"Bet you didn't know that Martin Luther King, Samuel L. Jackson, and Spike Lee went to Morehouse College," Porsche said.

"Bet you didn't know I throw bitches out the car for talking too much," Blake fired back.

Porsche cracked up laughing. "Boy, you know I can't stand your black ass."

"I went to school. I ain't dumb, you know."

"Just thought all this Kush might have fried your brain cells. You never know. A lot of rappers nowa-days are dumb as a box of rocks. Can't even spell most of the stuff they say."

"Tell me somethin' about Spelman."

"All I know is the girl that played Rudy Huxtable on "The Cosby Show" went there. I didn't do no stud-ying about it or nothin', just know a li'l bit. Google can teach you some thangs." Her eyes went wide suddenly as she was looking at her smartphone. "Oh, my God. You are not going to believe this."

He waited for her to continue.

"That crazy ass dude Chief Keef just made it to Atlanta, so you know it's about to go down."

"Let me see that." Blake snatched the phone from her hand and gazed at it in disbelief. Chief Keef had just posted a new picture to

Instagram. It was a picture of him arriving at Hartsfield Jackson Atlanta Interna-tional Airport with his GBE squad in tow.

"Why are y'all beefing in the first place? I thought you liked his music? I remember you used to stay bumpin' that Love Sosa."

The beef had started all because Blake had collaborated with Atlanta's newest hip hop group Migos, shortly after they had begun a

Twitter war with the Chicago drill rapper, but Blake wasn't about to explain all that to Porsche's nosey ass.

He gave her the phone back. He wanted to call someone, but he could think of nothing to say and no one to say it to. After all, what was he going to say? That Chief Keef had followed him to Atlanta? That he suspected something might go down tonight? He knew that his team was ready to shoot just like he knew Sosa's team was ready to shoot. There was really nothing to say. In situations like that, he knew that actions were a hell of a lot more important than words. He mashed out the blunt, took another gulp from his drink, and shook his head.

"Next they gon' be saying T-Walk—"

"Shit," Porsche interrupted, "T-Walk is here too! They're plotting on you, Blake! You can't tell me no different. Ain't no way in hell both of these dudes just happen to show up in Atlanta on the night of your concert.

They're up to something."

A simple nod was all he gave. Porsche was right. He knew it. A quick Instagram check confirmed that T-Walk was in fact in Atlanta as well.

They were sending a message. A threat. And Blake did not take well to threats.

Chapter 25

Trintino "T-Walk" Walkson and his fiancée Ashley "Thunder" Hunter posed for a picture as soon as they made it into the airport, and he made sure that his number one goon Gusto wasn't in the photo before uploading it to Instagram. He couldn't risk having his main shooter being seen with him. He planned to get rid of Blake once and for all; he also planned to get away with it.

Ashley was driving a dark blue Escalade rental, and T-Walk was next to Gusto in the seat behind her as they cruised down Martin Luther King Jr Drive and turned right onto Northside Drive, circling the Georgia Dome. Cars were lined up for blocks, clear signs that an elite performer was in town, and the numerous Ferraris, Lamborghinis, Bentleys, and Benzes that were pulling up were no doubt Bulletface's industry friends. Millionaire rappers and singers, producers and label execs, actresses and actors, NFL and NBA stars, and more than likely a few billionaires who could afford to blow money like Blake and Alexus.

"Can't believe they wacked folks n'em," Gusto muttered. Clad in an expensive blue Pelle and Prada en-semble, he was like an angry bear; big and mean and ready to fight. Thanks to T-Walk, he had a rose gold Rolex watch on his left wrist that was replete with large round blue diamonds. The blue diamond necklace draping down his chest had a six-pointed star pendant with a large black diamond-encrusted G in the center of it. It signified his loyalty to the Gangster Disciples, though all who knew him would tell you that he'd even killed a few of his own gang members. He was a Gary, Indiana savage, a hotheaded gangster who didn't give a fuck about anybody who wasn't a GD.

"We gon' catch that nigga today," T-Walk said. "For the folks." "On Bernard," Gusto agreed.

"We was supposed to get Blake out the way a long time ago. Can't believe I didn't get him that one night behind the club. That nigga got God on his side."

"Don't trip, bruh. We catch him out here tonight we slidin'.

Everybody wit' him gotta go." Strapped into the shoulder holster beneath Gusto's left arm was a Glock 27 with a 50-round drum magazine.

T-Walk had a similar weapon in his own shoulder holster. "I'm emptyin' the whole fifty," he said. "Fuck trying to catch him at this concert. You know he gon' hit the strip club tonight. All we got to do is wait. We gotta make sure we get that nigga, bruh. Can't let him live after he shot the guys up. As soon as I catch him, he gets it. That's it that's all."

"I really want to whack Alexus. I'll never forget that night she shot me. I can't go out like that. She got to get it too."

T-Walk shook his head no. "She's the money tree. I can't let nothing happen to her. We'll get everything we need from her as long as we get Blake. With him dead, we'll be able to take over the cartel. It'll be too easy for me to get Alexus back. She still loves me. It's just that nigga Blake. He's in the way."

"Like you said, bruh. We got to catch him after the concert. He'll be at a strip club somewhere in the city. We'll find out where he's at as soon as he gets there."

T-Walk's eyes went back to his tinted window. He thought back to when he and Alexis had been togeth-er, back when he had really been rich. He still had millions in the bank and several more M's in dirty money stashed away inside his numerous residences throughout the country, but there was a limit to his money— unlike Alexus and Blake's.

"She was supposed to be my wife. That bitch got about a hundred billion dollars, no bullshit. If it weren't for me, she wouldn't have none of that shit. I'm the one who made those reality shows. "Brickhouse of Jupiter Island" and "North Palm Beach" were my ideas. That African American beauty pageant was my idea, and a bunch of the other shows too. She's getting rich off me. You're right. I should kill her ass too."

"Just give me the word, bruh. You know I'm goin'. And if Chief Keef and them GBE niggas catch her before we do, we might not even have to put in no work."

T-Walk shifted his attention to Ashley and told her to head to Magic City. He had a million dollars in cash with him; he would hit the club, pop a hundred black bottles, make it rain on the strippers, and wait.

King Rio

Chapter 26

It was almost a blur to Bulletface; over 71,000 crazed fans, screaming and cheering and smiling at him as he rapped into his diamond encrusted microphone. That night he was due to make a cool $10,650,000, which was much more than most rappers made in an entire year. But he wasn't your average rapper. He was Bulletface, the self-proclaimed king of the Midwest, the wealthiest rap star in history, and simultaneously the most dominant gangsta rapper in hip-hop. He'd already gone platinum several times since his debut album dropped years earlier. His record label boasted some of the industry's most revered talents.

To an extent, he had done what Bryan "Birdman" Williams had done with Cash Money Records, only he had done it in record time with Alexus's help. Now, he purchased Mercedes Maybachs, Rolls Royce Phantoms, and Bugatti Veyrons like white tees. Now, he had all his family and friends driving around in foreign cars, soaring from state to state in private jets, flossing the most brilliant of diamonds, buying homes that previously they would never have dreamed of owning. Social media had recently christened him "Baby Diddy" due to his immense wealth. The streets loved him because he was still a street guy, a gangsta rapper like Yo Gotti and Lil Boosie, and because his wife was as bad as Maliah and about a thousand times wealthier than any other black woman in the world was.

Five black diamond chains were tangled around his dark brown neck. He wondered if his diamond teeth were shining under the incessant flashes of smartphone cameras. He wore a pair of Louis Vuitton sunglasses to shield his eyes from the bright explosions of light, and the shades went along perfectly with his LV belt, sneakers, and the bandana that was hanging from the rear left pocket of his True Religion jeans. He was performing "Trap King," a track off his latest album, "Took the Throne."

'It's Arm and Hammer, like Kevin Gates Grab the pot let me demonstrate

Whip it with the fork let me penetrate I'm counting cash I don't snitch or play

Me and my hittas got white blocks, don't give a fuck about white cops

Sell white all night and day nigga

And we strapped up; we don't fight opps

Racked up, sellin' 8 balls by the pool totin' that stick, nigga Try to rob me or snatch my chain bet a fuck nigga get hit nigga In this street shit, I'm the big boss

Dope Boy...Rick Ross

My amigos got a ton of bricks

And I'll buy it all, fuck what the shit cost

Bulletface, let fullys spray, sneak diss me I'm gon' pull a K Pull up like bang bang bang bang, shoot you all in the face Whippin' white, yola nigga

You only live once, YOLO nigga Can't trust a soul so we solo nigga Dolo nigga, don't know no nigga...'

Young Meach, Will Scrill, P.A.T., and Mocha were on the stage with Blake, as well as several other mem-bers of his MBM team. Jeezy and Wayne were scheduled to come out next. In the front row close to the stage, Blake spotted Atlanta Housewives stars NeNe Leakes and Porsha Williams.

K. Michelle, KeKe Palmer, Kim Kardashian, Ciara, and LaLa Anthony weren't far from them.

Blake moved to the right of the stage, steadily scanning the crowd as he continued his performance. He spotted a group of young guys with dreadlocks and grim expressions staring at him. They were the only close spectators that weren't excited.

Their cold glares made Blake's heart drum in his chest.

He knew then that it would be a perilous night. Though he and his gang had enough guns to battle any group of young gangsters, he was still nervous. Too much was at stake. He would kill before he'd let anyone try and take his life. He'd been shot— numerous times — and the idea of getting shot again didn't sit too well.

After completing the song, he performed with the rap gods, and then performed another song that fea-tured Diddy and Jay Z titled "Black Kings."

Just as expected, the crowd roared when Hove and Diddy joined him on the stage. He'd been standing in front of his black Bugatti Veyron

Super Sport when the two titans drove up behind him in their own black Bugattis and emerged holding twin bottles of their own liquors, Ace of Spades and Ciroc.

Bulletface sailed into his verse as soon as the beat dropped.

'Nigga, I'm the king, fuck you mean? Name a nigga who can fuck wit me Got hittas they'll light you up for free Mansions all in my custody Diamonds on my neck clustering Hop out the Veyron and tuck the heat I can't go for no fuckery

Fuck all y'all niggas, don't fuck wit' me Coast to coast in that G6, G5 still street shit

The way we ride you should peep this, Young Al Capone o' dis street lit.

Think I'm Donald, but I ain't goin' Pole on me now think I ain't blowin'?

Got me feelin' like Tip, ridin' round, long clips...sneak dis me and I'm on it.

One phone call you a goner Maybach Landaulet, I'm the owner.

Got the whole Springfield, think I'm Homer Trap house roamer, Lean Styrofoamer

Boutta buy the Bulls and the Bears, nigga, I ain't got a care It's just me and my money; I'm a loner

Smoke big dope, I'm a stoner

Got the baddest bitch livin' and I'm on her

It's Dub Life Goons and Money Bagz gang till I'm muhfuckin' dead...it's over...gang'

As Hove began his verse, Blake decided to head back to the side of the stage and eye his enemies. They were still as stone-faced as they'd been a few moments earlier.

He raised his heavy diamond chains in his fist and gave an open-mouthed snarl to show his diamond teeth. He was the king of hip-hop, what he believed Pac would be if he were still here. He wasn't afraid of a soul.

Neither was his MBM team.

When they caught sight of the Glo Gang, they mobbed over and formed a semicircle around Blake, most of them chugging bottles of Ace of Spades and Ciroc, holding stacks of hundreds, and throwing up gang signs. Like their CEO, they were all swagged in black Pelle and Louis Vuitton (the LV logos symbolizing their loyalty to the Vice Lords) with gleaming gold chains and Rolex watches.

The Glo Gang was unfazed by MBM's show of bravado, and Blake knew why: they were members of one of the most ruthless street gangs in Chicago; nothing fazed them, not even bullets.

Blake shifted his attention back to Hove, then to the seemingly endless panorama of diverse faces in the crowd. There were whites, blacks, Hispanics, Asians, and everything in between. Thousands of turnt up men and women, all rapping along to the songs. He appreciated the sight of Atlanta's elite celebs in front of the stage.

To himself, he thought, I'm the king of this shit, and the thought made him smile.

The concert lasted well over two hours. It was midnight by the time Blake and Porsche made it back in-side the Ferrari. She fixed him a cup of Lean and rolled up a stogie of loud as he sped off ahead of his MBM team's sparkling fleet of foreigns. They were all headed to Onyx for the official Bulletface concert after party.

"This is the life right here," Porsche chirped merrily as she sipped from a water bottle.

Blake gave the bottle a look of scrutiny. "The fuck you drinkin'?" he asked. "Water."

Porsche didn't even sound believable. The strong stench of hard liquor was on her breath. Blake had lost track of her at the concert, and he figured she had gone back stage with the other rappers.

"Stop lyin'. That ain't no water."

"It is water. You need to get off my case. I'm grown." "You ain't grown enough."

"Yes, I am. You just ain't got a chance to see it yet."

"Yeah, a'ight." Blake kept flicking his eyes in every direction. He'd heard nothing more about T-Walk and Chief Keef.

Their whereabouts concerned him.

"Blake, I'm hungry. Can you stop at Fat Matt's Rib Shack? It's right on Piedmont. We'll pass it before we get to Onyx."

"It's open this late?"

"Yeah, boy." Her voice was suddenly seductive, and Blake found himself ogling her pretty glossed lips again. She'd changed into a form- fitting black tube dress and black Louboutin heels with gold spikes that complemented her expensive gold jewelry. The dress barely covered four inches of her luscious dark thighs. Blake's eyes fell briefly to them before he shook his head and remembered who she was.

He took a few swallows of the Promethazine, Codeine, and Sprite mix and smoked like a chimney. His eyes returned to the road.

"I know what you want, Blake," Porsche murmured. "You can get it too. All you gotta do is ask. You ain't never heard that before? Ask and you shall receive."

"Don't start that crazy shit. I ain't on that."

"I heard you got a big old humongous dick too."

Blake chuckled at the lascivious comment and said nothing.

"Boy, you know I won't tell nobody. I'm grown enough to keep my mouth shut, since you want to talk about me being grown. Bet I can do some grown thangs with this pussy."

Again, he remained silent. He had the right to remain silent. He was a newly married man, and going against his vows was not on his to-do list. He had to admit, though, Porsche was a beautiful dark-skinned young woman. She definitely had sex appeal. He thought back to when he had first met her and remembered how incredibly sexy she'd looked in those tiny boy shorts. Numerous times since then he'd found himself staring at her whenever she was in the same room. But of course, he could not do what the single Blake would have done.

A screech of tires shifted his attention back to the street just as he was turning onto Piedmont.

It was a blue Escalade and a white Audi, both peeling away as masked gunmen hung out the passenger side windows with assault rifles and opened fire on the MBM gang's refulgent fleet of matte black whips.

Bullets were pinging into the Ferrari's hood as Blake snatched the Mac-11 off his lap and hopped out with his finger already squeezing the trigger. A round flitted past his left ear. Out of the corner of his eye, he saw Meach, Scrill, Rube, P.A.T., and Batman shooting at the escaping gunmen as the Audi and Escalade disappeared down Rockledge Road.

When Blake turned to check on his team, he found P.A.T. lying in the middle of the street with a bullet wound in the bridge of his nose.

The back of his head was wide open and a mess of mushy brain matter was piled near his frozen face.

P.A.T. was dead.

Chapter 27

"I hate the summer time. Niggas always shootin'. Dumb asses killin' each other when they should be on these police for lockin' 'em all up and treatin' 'em any kinda way," Porsche complained bitterly.

She gazed down at Blake with her hands on her hips. They were back at his Atlanta home. She had con-vinced him to let her drive after the shooting, and he'd been out of it shortly thereafter. Instead of hitting the strip club, they had all headed to his place, and he'd gone straight to his bedroom.

Porsche had followed.

He was stretched out on the bed, gazing up at the ceiling with intoxicated eyes. Porsche had slipped some crushed Molly pills and a Xanax bar into his Lean as they had left the concert, and now he was halfway unconscious. A sliver of drool crept out from the corner of his mouth and made its way down the side of his face. He spoke in a near whisper.

"I'm sooooo high. On King Neal...I'm on Mars right now."

"I can tell." Porsche stepped out of her heels and walked over to shut and lock the bedroom door. "I've always loved you, Bulletface. You know that?" She climbed onto his lap, pulled off her tube dress, and showed him that she'd been nude under it. She grabbed his hands and put them on her small breasts. "You fucked Rihanna, didn't you? Ain't I sexy and slim like her?"

"You...trip—" and just like that he nodded off.

Porsche smiled and applied a long, juicy wet French kiss to his lips.

She stood up at the foot of the bed and hastily stripped him of his clothes. An audible gasp escaped her throat as she peeled down his Versace underwear and got a look at his long black pole.

"Damn! I knew it was gon' be big," she curled the fingers of one hand around it, slurped the large head into her mouth, then popped it out, "but I didn't think it would be this damn big. I gotta record this. We can have our own sex tape! Porsche and Bulletface."

She kissed him again, then put her purse on his chest and set her smartphone against it so she could rec-ord the moment she got to taste him.

The doorknob shook suddenly.

"Blake, what's up, bruh? You good?" Meach shouted from outside the door. There was a second door-knob struggle. "Bruh, everybody just pulled up. I mean everybody. Every celebrity in town. You need to get out here, bruh. They came to make sure you was good."

"He's asleep, Meach," Porsche said, nervously hitting record on the smartphone.

She clamped her hands around the base of his dick and began stroking it up and down.

"Why the fuck you in there if he sleep?" Meach asked, and for a second Porsche thought her plan had been ruined. Then Meach added, "We'll be downstairs in the studio all night. Tell bruh to come down there," and he left without another word.

With a conniving smirk, Porsche slapped Blake across the face. Two more slaps and his eyes cracked open.

"Baby," he murmured.

"I'm here, Bulletface," Porsche replied as she took his length in her mouth and began sucking it.

He got hard almost instantly. Porsche licked at the sides, slathering his long black pole in spit. She stroked and sucked him. Squeezed his heavy scrotum in her other hand. Teased the head of his dick with her flickering tongue. After all the practice she'd had in Chicago, she was practically a certified head doctor. She took him to the back of her throat and left the majority of his length wedged there for a couple of seconds before slurping it back out and continuing to fellate him. She grabbed the smartphone and turned it to his face just as he was shutting his eyes again.

He grunted twice and muttered, "Damn."

She put the camera back on herself and sucked her favorite rapper until he blew his load in her mouth. She quickly got him hard again, and this time she mounted him and rode him, changing positions, moaning, biting the center of her lower lip, and pinching her nipples. Blake was awake but unresponsive, unmoving; his only sign of life was an occasional grunt.

"Mmm...I love you, Bulletface. You love me back, don't you? I'm your wife, nigga. Say that shit," Por-sche said between moans. "I'm in love with you, Blake. I'll always be in love with you. I'ma make you stop looking at me as a little girl. I bet you loving this pussy now, ain't you? Look at you. That's the good pussy face you making."

She giggled and kept right on riding him, lost in the moment. She'd wanted to give him some since be-fore she had ever met him, and now that his dick was deep inside her, she decided that it was well worth the wait.

King Rio

Chapter 28

Alexus stepped out of her pearl white Rolls Royce Phantom Drophead Coupe, shouldered her white croc skin Birkin bag, and looked at all the cars that were parked in front of her and Blake's Atlanta home. She had her iPhone 6 Plus in hand. She donned a snow-white Chanel mini dress and white leather peep-toe pumps.

"Why is this black bastard not answering his phone?" she muttered through clenched teeth.

Enrique shrugged dismissively; Flako and Pedro didn't comment; Mercedes stormed past everybody and headed inside.

"Mercedes," Alexus said, trailing her sister inside, "you better pray that I don't have to fuck your sister up today. I am so serious."

In the foyer, they ran into Meach. He was holding an AK 47 and smoking a blunt, mumbling something into his cell phone. He looked up from the phone and shook his head at Alexus. His eyes were dark red.

Stressed.

"P got killed," he said, and the news brought tears to Alexus's eyes. "What? Oh, my God. When did this happen? Is Blake okay? Where is he?"

"Upstairs. Said he was goin' to sleep. Porsche up there with him.

Think he might have drunk too much Lean. Smoked too much Kush or somethin'."

Alexus and Mercedes exchanged questioning looks, and then Alexus excused herself and started up the staircase, pulling her .50-caliber Desert Eagle out of her Birkin bag and glaring back at Mercedes, who quickly rushed up the stairs behind her.

"Whatever happens," Mercedes pleaded urgently, "don't shoot my sister. She's all I have left, Alexus."

"I'm not tryna hear that shit! If she is in here doing anything with my man, it's going down."

Their expensive heels click-clacked on the glass stairs. Alexus felt her heartbeat quicken as she ascended the staircase. She glued her eyes to the master bedroom suite's door...just as Porsche came walking out of another bedroom further down the hallway.

She was wrapped in a bath towel, hair hidden inside a shower cap, and she seemed just as surprised as Alexus.

"Where is Blake?" Alexus got right to the point. Porsche looked at the gun, and her eyes went wide.

"He in there asleep."

"Explain to me why you are half dressed in the house with my man when I'm not here."

"Girl, I wanted to take a shower! Damn, a bitch can't take a shower now?"

Alexus squinted. Thoughtfully, she walked to the bedroom door and cracked it open. Blake was indeed asleep. He was tucked beneath the covers, lying on his side facing the door, a sliver of saliva dangling down from the side of his face. The blanket was up to his neck. His jewelry was on the bedside table, his guns on an easy chair in the corner.

Shutting the door, she turned to Porsche. Gave another squint. She wanted to choke Porsche for no rea-son other than the fact that she was there alone with Blake.

"No more of this kind of shit. From now on, no hanging around my husband if I'm not here. I will cut a bitch about mine, you understand me? Quick too. No hesitation."

Porsche displayed an innocent smile. "It's not that deep, Lexi. P just got killed. I was there. This shit is crazy for me too."

"Oh, you ain't seen crazy." Alexus tucked the gun back down in her purse. "Don't let me catch you doing this again. You were supposed to be setting up the bachelorette party, that's it. I don't know how the hell you ended up here with Blake. If it happens again, we got problems.

Comprende?"

Porsche rolled her eyes and returned to the bedroom she'd just stepped out of. Alexus looked at Mer-cedes.

"Don't look at me! I was with you."

"If you love her, you better tell her to stay the fuck away from what's mine. Not unless you're trying to be without a baby sister."

Shaking her head and crossing her arms, Mercedes joined Porsche in the bedroom and slammed the door shut.

King Rio

Chapter 29

"We got them niggas," T-Walk said with a chuckle as he tossed a stack of dollar bills at a stripper and turned up his gold bottle.

He and Gusto had participated in the shooting that took P.A.T.'s life, and GBE had aided them by open-ing fire from their rented Audi on orders from Chief Keef.

T-Walk and his fellow GDs were fifty deep in the VIP section at Onyx, throwing fistfuls of cash at big-bootied strippers as they twerked and pussy-popped in front of them.

One stripper in particular had T-Walk's full attention. Her stage name was Cakez, but she'd told him that her real name was Monica. It was no secret that Trintino "T-Walk" Walkson was one of the most successful television producers in the industry, which was why he was never surprised when bad bitches like Cakez showed him special attention at the strip clubs.

Ashley didn't get jealous. She always stood next to him at the strip clubs, just as she was doing then, slapping, and squeezing Cakez's ass and drinking from her own bottle of Ace of Spades. She was voguish in a light blue Gucci bodysuit that put her enormous derriere on full display. Blue diamond jewelry shone on her neck, ears, and wrists. She was T-Walk's queen; she stayed fly.

"On the BOS," Gusto said, "I knew we was gon' catch one of 'em.

Just wish it would've been Blake. I was cool wit' Pat. Did time wit' dat nigga. He was solid, straight dope boy. But fuck dat nigga. He shouldn't have been wit' dem niggas. Opp ass muhfucka."

He curled one of his massive black arms around the stripper who was dancing for him and pulled her back against his crotch.

The girl frowned and yanked away from him. "No touchin'!" she snapped.

"Bitch, stop trippin'. I'm throwin' all this muhfuckin' money; I'ma touch what the fuck I wanna touch."

She made the worst mistake she could have possibly made. She turned and spit in Gusto's face.

He swung a swift hook at her jaw, and T-Walk heard the bones in her face crack as Gusto's heavy fist knocked her unconscious.

Everyone who saw the brutal knockout punch froze. T-Walk grabbed Gusto; B.O. and Aaron, two of T-Walk's cousins, helped him pull Gusto toward the rear exit before security could reach him.

"Man, folks! The fuck you do that for?" T-Walk asked incredulously. "Bitch spit in my face."

"Folks, you gotta chill—"

Suddenly, gunshots boomed from somewhere in the club, silencing Trintino as he and his entourage spilled out the back door. Chips of drywall and paint flew into his face.

The bullets were flying at him.

"That's them MBM niggas!" somebody shouted.

T-Walk was stumbling out the door behind Gusto when he felt a splash of blood on his face.

Gusto collapsed into the parking lot with a hole in the back of his head. T-Walk nearly tripped over Gus-to as he rushed to safety.

"That was that nigga Rube shootin', G! He shot folks!" B.O. shouted as they rushed to the Escalade. "They killed big folks!"

T-Walk didn't speak. He looked at the club and watched as everyone ran outside, screaming and hollering about the shooting. Ashley was next to him. One of her heels had broken in her haste to keep up, but otherwise she was okay.

The way he looked at it, his team was taking a helluva lot more losses than Blake's team. And he was sick of it. Sooner or later, he thought, Blake is going to die, and I'll be the man pulling the trigger.

Police sirens blared in the distance.

T-Walk reclined in the passenger seat and Ashley sped off down Cheshire Bridge Road with her hands trembling on the steering wheel.

"This war between you and Blake really needs to stop. Neither side is winning. We've already lost Li'l Ant, and now look at Gusto. It won't stop until you're dead or Blake is dead, and I can't take the pressure of knowing that it might be you."

"Don't worry about me. I got me. Just drive and let me do the thinking."

"I'm only giving my opinion."

"Do I look like I give a damn about somebody's opinion? My nigga just got shot in the head back there." He turned and looked out the back window. His cousins were following close behind them in a black Escalade. "We need to find out where that nigga stay out here in Atlanta. Then we can just come through and finish this shit once and for all."

"Don't you still have Mercedes's phone number? Call and ask her where the hell he staying. I'm pretty sure she'll know. Hell, you know she can't stand his ass anyway. She'll be quick to give up his address, as long as she's not in harm's way."

T-Walk shook his head. He was wiping the blood from his face with a paper towel. "Their security is serious. Ain't no way in hell I'll be able to get past all those Mexican bodyguards that Alexus keeps around."

"Well, there has to be some way. We can't just keep letting this go on the way it is. Sooner or later we'll all be dead fuckin' around with those damned Costillas, and that is not a road that I'm trying to travel."

"Drive, baby. Let me think. I'll figure something out. I always do, don't I?"

Ashley gave no reply. She kept her eyes on the road and drove. No music. No phone interruptions. Just steady mileage to get them away from the murder that had just taken place at Club Onyx.

T-Walk fired up a blunt. "Rest in peace, big folks. Damn." He inhaled and exhaled, inhaled and exhaled, gazing up at the sunroof, wondering if, like the rest of his guys, he would die by the gun at the hands of Blake's goons. He didn't want to die, but he definitely wasn't afraid to die.

King Rio

Chapter 30

Blake was groggy when he woke up the following morning.

Extremely groggy. More tired and disoriented than he could ever remember being.

The memory of Pat's murder came to him first. Then the concert and Porsche leaving with him. Then...

"Good morning, bae," Alexus said.

He turned and looked at her. She was under the heavy white covers with him, staring at his face with her brows furrowed, rolling his earlobe between a thumb and forefinger.

"The fuck you doin' here? Shit, what time is it?" He yawned and turned to her. She pecked her lips against his.

"Almost noon. What made you go to sleep butt naked? Tell me that first. Then tell me what the hell hap-pened with Pat."

"To keep it a hundred, baby, I don't even remember going to sleep. I must've took a shower. I don't know. I was too high."

"Hmm."

"Damn, man."

"What happened to Pat?" "Fuck you think happened?"

"Don't take your anger out on me. It's not like I shot him. And what do you mean you must have taken a shower? You don't remember if you took a shower or not?"

He shook his head groggily and glanced at the wide-screen Apple Smart TV on the wall across from the foot of the bed. It was on MTN News, one of the many cable channels owned by Costilla Corp.

Pat's murder was big news, but the Trump suicide bombing and the Lake Shore Drive attacks on Alexus were top stories that hardly went a minute without being mentioned. ISIS in America was another unsettling topic.

Even more unnerving was Alexus's expression: tight and studious, her green eyes squinted, her brows pushed close together. She was suspicious of something— Blake was certain of it. He just didn't know what she was thinking, or what he might have done wrong. His mind was too clouded to think of anything.

"So, uuuuuhhh, what did you and Porsche do last night?" And there went the lightbulb.

"What?" he sat up in bed and looked down at her. "Don't start with that bullshit. Let a nigga wake up first. Get me some breakfast or somethin' before you start interrogating me."

"I just want to know. It seems mighty suspicious that you were here with her, and you don't even re-member what happened. Yes, I do have a problem with my man being butt ass naked in the bed when I get here if he was here with another woman. That shit irritates me. I want to know what's going on. What happened? Let me in on the little secret."

Blake shook his head. He got out of bed, thinking of Pat and last night's shooting.

"Ain't no fuckin' secret," he said. "My nigga got killed last night.

Don't come in here accusing me of this bullshit. Where the fuck is my breakfast? Huh? Tell me that se-cret."

"I'm sorry to hear about what happened to Pat, but that ain't got nothing to do with you being butt naked and smelling like you just got out the tub. I'm telling you now, Blake, if you fucked that bitch, I'm going to kill you and her. Think I'm playing if you want to."

Blake decided not to speak again until he had some food in his stomach. He went to the bathroom and showered. Alexus stood outside the shower and watched him, arms crossed, still squinting. When he made it back to the bedroom minutes later, a delicious breakfast of shrimp and grits awaited him. He ate in silence. He felt dizzy, yet he didn't remember doing anything extra the previous night. All he had done was smoke some loud and drink some Lean, but it felt like he'd popped a thousand pills.

He put on a white Louis Vuitton outfit with matching Louboutin sneakers and then added his bulletproof vest, five white diamond necklaces, and a white diamond Rolex watch, all the time trying to remember what had happened after the shooting. No matter how hard he tried, nothing came to mind.

"Atlanta PD was here to talk to you about Pat's murder," Alexus said, standing before him with her arms crossed as he ate. "I told them I'd have you call them later. I think they want you to come down to the station for questioning."

"I ain't got nothin' to say. I didn't see shit," he spoke with a full mouth.

"It's not really about what you saw. They're investigating. You know how investigations go. Just go down there and see what they want. You'll be out of there in no time."

He shook his head no. "I ain't goin'. Fuck that. If I go anywhere it'll be to catch them niggas who did that shit."

"You're too late for that. Your guys already shot up Onyx about that last night. One of T-Walk's guys was killed. A few other people were shot too. It all went down right around the time I got here."

Instinctively, he grabbed his smartphone to check the text messages and saw that Rube had sent him sev-eral texts concerning the club shooting. Apparently, T-Walk's right hand man had been killed in retaliation for Pat's murder. Judging from the text alone, Rube had been the shooter.

There were a bunch of other texts regarding the death of one of hip- hop's most well-known rappers. News of Pat's murder had already reached World Star Hip Hop, Media Take Out, and TMZ. He was the third MBM rapper to be gunned down in the past two years alone.

"Get your eyes off the phone and pay attention to the TV." Alexus turned up the television volume. "ISIS is tearing Mexico to pieces. We were able to catch a few groups of them before they made it to us, but there are way too many of them. We are in danger, Blake. I mean serious danger. I don't even know if our kids are safe. Those terrorists could be in the United States any day now. You saw what they did to us in Chicago. Just imagine if there were dozens and dozens of them. What do we do then?"

Blake didn't know what to say. He missed the good old days when all he did was sit in a crack house and sell dope all day. Nowadays the world was too dangerous. Terrorists, rap beefs, and his ongoing beef with T- Walk — it was all too much. He wanted to take his wife and kids and fly back to Spain where they spent their honeymoon. Anywhere but the United States.

"There's something else that has me worried," Alexus said. She sat down next to him and massaged his shoulders. "I'm really starting to think that my uncle Flako is out to get me. I know that may sound crazy, but I'm telling you it's the truth. I can tell just by looking at him that he's up to something. Pedro wants to tell me, but I think he's too afraid."

"You shouldn't have taken over all those cartels. You was doing just fine with just the Costilla cartel. Now you run all of Mexico, so of course you gon' have to deal with what comes with it. You knew how those cartels got down before you decided to take over. Don't get scared now."

"I'm not scared. I'm just telling you what's going on. I see the situations for what they are. We're dealing with more enemies than probably anybody in the world. I don't know if it's safe to stay here in the US or Mexico. That island may not even be safe enough."

"Just stay with me. I told you I'll keep us safe. You know I ain't gon' let nothin' happen to us or the kids," Blake said, setting his plate aside and gulping down a glass of iced orange juice. He was unusually warm, and he was still finding it difficult to think straight. "Damn," he rubbed the ball of his hand over his eyes and yawned. "Feel like I got drugged or somethin'.

Damn. I ain't never been this tired before. For real, though." He heard his wife gasp.

At the same moment, the idea registered with him.

"If that hoe drugged you..." Alexus murmured, her eyes widening.

That's when Blake remembered Porsche's flirtatious comments on the way home from the concert, and her fixing his cup of Lean after the concert.

He stood up quickly.

"Where the fuck Porsche at?" he asked, wearing the same look of suspicion that Alexus had worn mo-ments earlier.

Alexus got up and left the room. Seconds later, she returned and said, "She's gone to the island. Enrique said they just left about twenty minutes ago."

"I'm fuckin' that bitch up if I find out she put somethin' in my drank."

"Oh, you won't even have to touch her. I'll do that myself. And that's a promise," Alexus said.

King Rio

Chapter 31

Alexus had on a white T-shirt that read "The Baddest," across the chest and a pair of white sweatpants; she lost the sweats and pushed Blake onto the bed. His veiny black hands grabbed and squeezed her derriere as she sat on his lap and planted a passionate kiss on his lips. Her Clive Christian's Imperial Majesty perfume— $215,000 a bottle— permeated the air and filled his nostrils with the most heavenly scent.

Her ass felt as soft as cotton in his hands. Her sitting on his lap with no panties on was the easiest way to get Blake's thick phallus erect and ready for a raucous episode of lovemaking. It never failed, and that time was no different.

His dick was like a pole beneath a tent, buttressing the crotch of his baggy LV sweatpants. He slipped his hands under her shirt and pushed it up over her head, kissing and licking her breasts as they became available.

"You are not about to fuck me without a condom," Alexus said, pushing him onto his back and remold-ing her mouth to his. "Ain't no telling what kinda drugs you got in you if she did dope you up. We need to get you a blood test ASAP to see what's in your system."

"You got some rubbers?" Blake asked, eager to slide into her lubricious nookie.

"Hell no, I don't have any rubbers, and you'd better not have any either!"

"I don't." Blake grinned and chuckled. He sucked her nipples and massaged her clit with his fingertips. "So I can't get none?"

"Not without a condom." "We're married."

"And?"

With a rapidly burgeoning smile, he pulled her thighs up his chest and inhaled deeply as her wet pussy met his lips. Alexus had the best- smelling juice box of the century. He sucked on her clitoris and watched her pinch her nipples and moan. Digging his tongue deep inside her, he rubbed his strong black hands on her thick thighs as she rode his face.

Then she did something she'd never done.

She turned around and grinded her asshole on his tongue.

The move caught him by surprise, but he got over it quickly and pulled her pillow-soft cheeks down onto his face. He licked and licked and licked, lost in her softness.

"Mmm," Alexus moaned. "We need to get you doped up more often."

Blake was definitely doped up. He felt the drugs in his system. It had him dizzy. He thought of the Lean Porsche had made for him and hoped that she hadn't pulled a "Hangover" move on him. Something had certainly happened. He wasn't feeling that drowsy from nothing.

Alexus was a professional undresser; she stripped him in seconds and began stroking his rigid pole in her hands.

He stopped licking. "The fuck you doin'?" he asked. "Start suckin'." "I'm not putting my mouth on you until I find out what happened

between you and Porsche."

Blake couldn't believe it. There he was licking her every hole and she didn't want to return the favor. But he had to admit she had a point.

"She could've got me too," he said. "She made my Lean after the show. I remember P gettin' killed, but I can't remember nothin' else."

"If she did that shit she's dead."

"Whether she did it or not, I still deserve to get some mouth and lip service."

"No the fuck you don't," Alexus scoffed. She sat up, turned to look down at him, and then dropped her juicy nookie down on his lips. "Shut up and eat this pussy. I should fuck you up for not paying attention. Stupid."

She slapped the top of his head, winding her hips.

Blake licked and licked and licked. His tongue danced on her clitoris, inside her sweet folds, and back to her clitoris again. His dick was as hard as steel, and he wanted to slam it in and out of her.

Tasting her juices and hearing her moans drove away the odd dizziness he'd been feeling since he woke up.

Soon she was shivering and gushing on his unrelenting tongue.

Massaging her nipples and whimpering. Gasping and panting. "See," she said with a breathless giggle as she hopped up and reached for her sweatpants, "that's why I married you right there. That kind of tongue will make any woman fall in love."

Blake sat up and frowned, stroking his python in both hands. "You better do somethin' to this dick."

Alexus laughed and pulled on her shirt. She blew him a kiss and headed for the door, smirking at his obvious discontent.

Someone began pounding on the door before she reached it. "Alexus," shouted Enrique. "Turn on the news. CNN."

Shaking his head, Blake dressed hurriedly and gritted his teeth at the protruding bulge in the crotch of his pants. He knew something serious was up. With the Costilla Cartel, you just never knew what was on the news.

It was bad news.

"...Airports in Houston, Dallas, Los Angeles, New York, and Chicago have been simultaneously at-tacked by groups of armed gunmen believed to be Islamic State militants. Up to four hundred are reported dead, and we're expecting the numbers to rise. Police agencies are still shooting it out with the gunmen. According to numerous eyewitnesses, the militants arrived at the airports at approximately 8 a.m. Eastern Time and immediately opened fire on any and every one."

"Meanwhile, other groups of gunmen have attacked a mansion owned by American billionaire Alexus Costilla in northern Mexico and MTN headquarters in Chicago. And we've just received word that video of Islamic militants beheading several MTN execs has been uploaded to Liveleaks, a website notorious for broadcasting the atrocities perpetrated by terrorist organizations. In the video, a masked man aims a knife at the camera and threatens Alexus Costilla before beheading four men and three women inside the MTN Tower. The full video is much too graphic to show, but here's a clip of the threat made against Alexus..."

Blake and Alexus did not breathe as the terrorist video started.

The man had a shiny bowie knife in his left hand. His head was wrapped in black cloth, leaving only his eyes visible in a narrow strip. His voice was raspy with a heavy Spanish accent.

"Drugs and greed is the scourge of the Americas. All your politicians are underhanded crooks, sexual deviants, and adulterers who steal from the poor to give to the rich. You worship money, drugs, and sex instead of worshipping Allah. You worship the darkness of society. You worship the underworld and by doing so you worship Alexus Costilla, the

queen of the underworld. Now America will fall because of it, and the men of the Islamic State will in-habit the earth as kings. We will win this Holy War. The West will suffer for its misdeeds. Alexus Costilla and her demons will suffer as well."

The video clip ended, and Blake saw his wife's face go pale.

He picked up his Mac-11 from the bedside table and tucked it in his pants, realizing then that the drama had only just begun. His smartphone rang as Alexus opened the door for Enrique. Pedro and Uncle Flako walked in behind him wearing matching white Hartmarx suits that were tailored to perfection.

"That's Juan Costilla talking," Pedro said. "Our long lost cousin." He puffed his cigar in an almost pride-ful manner. "Only someone in our bloodline could wreak such havoc. They're like Aunt Jenny reincarnated."

Blake answered the call from Meach, picking up his AK-47 from beside the nightstand.

"Bruh, all three of the stash houses just got hit. A bunch of niggas with dreadlocks and choppers. They hit us for everything, bruh, and killed most of the squad. It's fucked up. Damn near every one of our workers is dead or shot up. I don't know what to do, bruh. It's them GBE niggas. Shit crazy."

Blake shook his head and gritted his teeth cantankerously. He couldn't wait for his next trip to Chicago.

Chapter 32

"I have a confession," Porsche said as she sat across from her sister on the Gulfstream 650 private jet Alexus had bought for them four months prior.

Mercedes leaned forward, all ears.

"I put some pills in Blake's drink last night, and I fucked him on camera." Porsche said it as if there was nothing wrong with it.

"You're gonna get yourself killed, Porsche. Alexus is nobody to play with. I just watched her people behead about a hundred guys in Mexico."

"That boy needed some pussy. He's too stressed out. He really should have married a bitch like me. We some real hood bitches. Alexus was born with a silver spoon in her mouth. I take that back— a golden spoon. Blake the kind of nigga you and me grew up around, you know what I'm saying? He a real street nigga. Plus, he's a billionaire. Why the hell would I not give him this pussy?"

"You're messing up, little sis. You and I both know that Alexus is not about to play with you when it comes to Blake. She'll kill you and won't think twice about it. Where is the recording?"

"On my phone." "Give it here." "Hell no. It's mine."

"I just wanna see it. Remember Rihanna did that interview and said a gangsta rapper she fucked had the biggest dick she ever had? I wanna see if she was talkin' about him."

"Oh, she most definitely was." Porsche beamed as she found the video in her phone and hit play.

Mercedes watched it in stunned silence.

"See?" Porsche said. "Humongous. I couldn't believe it when I saw how big it was."

"You drugged that man," Mercedes said in disbelief. "Alexus is going to kill you."

"She ain't gon' find out. I didn't do nothin' but have a li'l fun with him. It ain't like he's cheating on her with me, you know?"

"How can you even rationalize this? You drugged him and raped him. Period. You're a rapist."

"I'm a damned good one."

Mercedes rolled her eyes and sighed. She twisted the diamond ring on her left hand's ring finger and wished her husband Kenny hadn't gone to the feds. She wanted to get away from all the craziness that came with being a Costilla and having one of the sluttiest little sisters in the world.

A text message from a 773 number she didn't know appeared in her smartphone. It read: 'This T, hit my line.'

She responded: 'I don't know you.' 'T-Walk.'

Her eyes widened. "I just got a text from T-Walk," she said, more to herself than to Porsche.

"Whaaaat? Wonder what the fuck he want."

"Nuh uh." Mercedes put the phone down and shook her head no. "I'm not about to be talking to him. Not with him and Blake beefing like that. All he going to want is for me to set him up again. You remember what happened last time. They shot up Blake's brand new Rolls Royce when he and Alexus were in it, right in front of the Versace Mansion. I'm not getting involved with him again."

"That was T-Walk who had Pat killed last night. I saw him on IG in the same Escalade right before the shooting. Some of Chief Keef's guys were driving around Atlanta in that white Audi. Everybody in the streets know what went down and who did what. They're at Blake's head. It might be a good thing I made that sex tape. He's famous and I'll probably have the only one around if he gets killed. Might make millions like Kim Kardashian and Ray J did. You never know."

"You need to delete that. I mean like right now. I'm telling you what's best for you, for us. I wouldn't be surprised if Alexus killed both of us about that sex tape. She's as crazy as Papi was. I see it now clear as day. We've already lost Mama, the kids, and Duke dealing with her and Blake...and that crazy ass Jenny Costilla. Delete that video before we both end up dead."

Porsche sucked her teeth and pulled the bundles of hundreds she'd gotten from Alexus out of her purse. "Let's focus on the setting up this bachelorette party for Alexus. We can have it on the island, have the strippers sent in on the jet. Give the pilots ten thousand for the extra flights; spend the other ninety on surprises. It'll be fun."

Mercedes spoke in an authoritative tone: "Delete the video."

Porsche stared at her big sister for a moment. Then she went to the video and deleted it. "There, you hap-py? It's gone."

"You're the one who should be happy. You're lucky to be alive after doing something to Blake. I'm seri-ous, li'l sister. Listen to me. Alexus and Blake are not to be fucked with. Yeah they're Hip-Hop's number one couple, but they're also the richest gangstas in America. Our best move would be to just play our role in the background and let them do them. Fucking around with them will get us killed, Porsche. Are you hearing me?"

Porsche gave a stubborn nod. "Damn, I said I deleted it." Mercedes looked out the circular window to her right and hoped

Alexus wouldn't be the death of her. True, she had everything a woman could want (especially with the $10,000,000 Alexus had wired to her account that morning), but the cost of being Alexus's sister far outweighed the pros. Nobody in the Costilla Cartel's inner circle was safe to be around. They were all just a bunch of filthy rich lunatics, and their enemies were just as much off their rockers.

"We're good, sis," Mercedes said. "They have islands for sale that will only cost a few million dollars. I'll get us one like Rita's. I like what she named that island. It's heaven spelled backwards."

"I bet it looks like heaven too."

"We'll see in"—Mercedes looked at her pink diamond and rose gold Rolex watch—"about 27 minutes. Maybe 30. Keep your damn mouth shut about that sex tape, and if anybody asks, you didn't give Blake anything.

You understand me?"

Porsche sighed and nodded.

Chapter 33

Rita was standing beside a white Range Rover limousine next to the runway with King Neal, Vari, and some bodyguards when Mercedes and Porsche's private jet landed. Ten minutes later, they were all in the limo and traversing a winding road lined with trees and armed guards.

The island sprawled along several miles of cliff top. Mercedes spotted a golf course; a large dock with a yacht, several boats and a bunch of workers unloading crates; a beach with sparkling white sands and a glorious view of the neighboring islands; and a hilltop mansion that looked like something taken straight from VH1's "The Fabulous Life of Filthy Rich Billionaires."

"Wow," Porsche said, gawking out her window. "This is some real Bill Gates type mess right here. You must have paid a grip for this place, Ms. Rita."

Vari said, "We all got our own bedrooms, and mine got Minnie Mouse all over the room. King got all wrestling stuff in his bedroom just like the one in Miami."

"I do," King confirmed, gawking out his own window. "Is my daddy and my momma on the way yet?"

"They'll be here in about an hour," Rita said.

Mercedes was admiring Rita's grey Gucci dress. It fit the middle- aged woman like a glove. She was a bit more curvaceous than Alexus and Mercedes, dark and stunningly beautiful with minimum jewelry and makeup, the epitome of modest for a billionaire like herself. Her hair was long and curly and parted down the middle. Her ever-present smile and soft Christian eyes settled Mercedes's nerves more than the two shots of Ciroc she'd had on the jet.

"Everything's going to be okay, baby," Rita said, patting Mercedes's

knee.

"I'm terrified," Mercedes said. "Luckily our plane took off before those terrorists hit the airport in Atlanta. They could have killed us if we had arrived 20 minutes later."

"Yeah, Alexus said she had to use the airport in Macon and get on Blake's jet because hers was stuck at that airport. I have prayed and prayed about this situation, Lord knows I have. I wish I'd known what kind of business Papi was involved in before I married him. I never would have put myself through this. I was a church going girl from Louisiana, never in my life even been around crime and criminals until I met the Costilla family."

"Makes me wish I would've never went to Britney Bostic's office to tell Alexus that I was her sister. I wasn't living the greatest life, but at least I wasn't living in danger."

"This all started with that damned Jenny. Everything went downhill after she found out that Alexus was the sole heiress to Vida Costilla's fortune. I was so glad when I heard that Jenny was dead. You don't understand all the pain she put me through. Especially when she killed Fred, my fiancé. Sometimes I thought I was literally in hell."

Mercedes nodded her head in agreement. "It's crazy."

"It most certainly is. But I'll tell you what. Nothing lasts forever. God will deliver us all from the evils of this planet. We'll walk among the angels. Alexus will too. Death is nothing to be afraid of. Not if you're saved."

Sure, Mercedes thought, already tired of the God talk. She looked at Porsche, who was busy playing digital Monopoly on an iPad with Savaria and King Neal. Then she looked down at the black-sequined Chanel dress she had on and thought of her own children, Baby Duke and Meyoncé Sky. The two were buried alongside their father's grave at Graceland Cemetery in Chicago. The children had been beheaded by the infamous Jenny Costilla. The father of Mercedes's children had been killed by some of Blake's associ-ates. Mercedes and Porsche's mother, Whitney Clark, had been killed by Alexus's team of hit men over Blake supposedly cheating with a girl named Whitney.

"Being a Costilla has ruined my life," Mercedes said finally. She toyed with her fingernails for a couple of seconds. "Ever since

I found out that your daughter was my sister, my life has been a living hell and a blessing at the same time. I mean, I always wanted money. I always wanted to be rich and wealthy, to drive the fastest, most expensive cars, and shit on

— sorry, Momma Rita, I meant stunt, like, flex, you feel me? To be on top of everybody. But look what it's cost me. My mother, my kids, the father of my kids, my own father, my cousin Bella who I hardly even knew. Now we're being targeted by terrorists. Blake's at odds with the craziest young nigga in the rap game. T-Walk wants him dead too. P.A.T. just got killed. Yellowboy got killed. Young D got killed. Bookie and Craig got killed. I feel like I'm living in a "Grand Theft Auto" video game, and it's not as fun as some people might think. Those losses hurt. I can't sleep some nights because of how much I miss my kids and my mama. It's just too much."

Mercedes didn't want to cry but she did anyway, endless crocodile tears that slid down her face like downhill skiers at an X Games event.

There was an open wound in her chest that would never heal. She knew it. Nothing, absolutely nothing, could be good enough to take the place of her now deceased family.

Rita leaned forward again and continued rubbing Mercedes's knee.

When King looked over and noticed his aunt's distraught expression, he scrambled over and gave her a hug.

"You okay, Auntie Cedes?" he inquired in a caring tone.

She smiled and rubbed his head. "I'm fine, King. I love yoooou." "I love you too, Auntie Cedes. Don't cry. Be happy." He kissed her

lips, smiled, and hugged her again. But that was all the time he had before his turn on the Monopoly game.

I'll live through this mess, Mercedes thought to herself. I'll be at the top with Alexus and Blake as long as I play my cards right. She looked at her sister. If only I could get this bitch to see the bigger picture.

King Rio

Chapter 34

The interior of Blake's private jet consisted mostly of polished mahogany and brown Louis Vuitton leather. Pacing a tight circle in the aisle between Alexus and her family and his MBM team, he was drinking a bottle of iced water and smoking a thick blunt of loud. Occasionally he glanced at his iced out watch, or his iPhone 6 Plus, or his beautiful wife as she sat in her seat reading an Ashley and Jaquavis novel on her Kindle tablet.

Just about everyone had sent him texts worried for him and his family and issuing their condolences for Pat. 2 Chainz, Scarface, 50 Cent, Jim Jones, Meek Mill, Rick Ross, Lil Durk, and T.I. were offering to lend their voices to squash his beefs with Chief Keef and T-Walk. Oprah said she was praying for him, as did Tyler Perry, Tika Sumpter, and Nicole Beharie. Denzel Washington offered a vacation at his plush estate in the Hamptons.

Gabrielle Union and D. Wade had essentially offered the same thing.

'This is a particularly trying time,' his music manager's text had read, 'but no time is too trying for Bullet-face. You will prosper through every tribulation. You are Blake King, a force to be reckoned with. Lay low. Call me later. I love you, young guy. You will live to a ripe old age. God isn't done with you. RIP P.A.T.'

The messages meant a lot to Blake, but his intentions to get rid of his enemies once and for all weighed heavier. He was a gangster, the epitome of a street nigga; he refused to back down from anyone.

"Boy, if you don't stop pacing back and forth like that," Alexus snapped. "Sit the fuck down some-where."

"These niggas got me fucked up, baby. On my son. I'm mothafuckin' Blake. I'm damn near the king of the mob! Fuck-niggas wanna keep playin' with me like it's a game. A'ight. I'ma give 'em somethin' to play with."

"Being all angry about it won't help. Actions speak louder than words. Sit down and think of what we can do next. Think of it as a chess game. What's your best move now?"

"Start shootin'."

Alexus laughed and rolled her eyes. "You're still as crazy as you were the day I met you. Don't you miss those old days? Remember how fat you were?" Another laugh. "Everything was good back then. All we did was fuck and blow money. We need to get back to that. We can't keep letting our enemies frustrate us like this. They are not going to go away anytime soon."

She put her reading tablet on the seat next to her, crossed her arms over her chest, and stared at Blake. "I can't focus on reading at a time like this. I can't believe they attacked all the airports. All this shit is getting out of hand. I wish Papi was still alive."

Meach had tears in his eyes. So did Scrill and Mocha. Pat had been like family to all of them.

Pedro and Flako were both stone-faced, studying the stock market on their iPads. Enrique was looking back and forth from Alexus to Blake and saying nothing. Like always, he was waiting to receive more orders from Alexus and pass them down to the Costilla cartel's underlings.

Mocha, the first lady of Money Bagz Management, was as beautiful as they came. She was a multiplati-num R&B songstress, slender and chocolate and as pretty as can be, dressed in a black Versace jumpsuit over Manolo pumps that displayed her impeccable red-painted toenails. She looked at Blake and said, "I quit. I give up. I'm leaving this business. I'll never record again for as long as I live. My voice died with Pat."

Blake had long suspected Pat and Mocha of secretly dating but he'd never heard anything to solidly prove it. Even then, he wasn't sure.

"You never give up, sis," Blake said. "We are going to win. We've already won, and we'll keep winning to the very end, you got that? I'm upset too, but quitting won't help. We just gotta overcome. That's the only option. Overcome and win. That's what winners do."

"Oh," Alexus said sarcastically, "now you wanna give good advice.

A minute ago you wanted to kill everything in sight." "I still do," he said.

"That's not the answer," Mocha said. Her lips were red like the polish on her toenails. "Enough is enough. We should be talking peace and prosperity. I'm so sick of this war it don't make no sense. Look at all the people we've lost. Yellowboy got killed fucking around with Chief Keef's crazy ass, and now the same thing just happened with Pat. I'm done, Blake. When we stop in Miami, I'm getting on another plane and flying off to Jamaica somewhere for at least a couple of months. I don't want any interviews, and I'm certainly not about to be doing any shows after my bro just got killed."

"Not to cut you off, Mocha," Alexus said, "but can somebody please tell me what the hell Porsche was doing in the bedroom with Blake last night? Why didn't anybody check on him?"

Meach frowned. "Check on him for what? We was just as fucked up about bruh getting killed as he was. And I did come up there to holla at Blake. Porsche said he was sleep."

"Think Porsche slipped somethin' in my cup," Blake said. "I can't even remember walking in the front door last night. It's like right after bruh got killed, my memory went black."

"And he wouldn't wake up when I got in bed with him," Alexus added.

A silent moment of group contemplation followed. It was Meach

who broke the silence.

"Damn. She was in there with you for a while too."

"Why the fuck would she drug you?" Scrill asked. "Think she wanted to fuck you that bad?"

Blake shrugged and passed Scrill the blunt. "I don't know. All I know is the Kush and Lean didn't do me like that. That was something else. I was drowsy as fuck this morning. Still am a li'l bit."

"Messed up if she date-rape-drugged you," Meach said.

His comment brought a sudden burst of laughter out of Scrill and Pedro. Flako grinned in amusement. Meach chuckled.

"Fuck all y'all," Blake said. He sat down across from Alexus as she joined in the laughter. "Fuck you, too," he said to her. "That shit ain't nowhere near funny."

"I told you not to trust that bitch. Did you forget about her trying to burn me to death in the tub that night? I told you she ain't to be trusted before you went to Atlanta with her. That's your fault."

"You ain't say shit."

"Yes, I did, and you know it."

Blake didn't like the smirks and giggles at his expense. He took in another gulp of water, mentally dis-secting the chain of events he was going through, and as his wife had suggested, thinking of his next move.

Which was when the idea struck him.

He picked up his smartphone and called Cup.

New York City

Cup was emerging from the rear of his shiny black armored Bentley Mulsanne on West 51st Street when his smartphone rang. Over the years, with savvy street investments — everything from kidnapping for ransom to dealing thousands of kilos of cocaine and heroin throughout his hometown of Chicago— he'd managed to accumulate over a hundred million dollars in dirty money and an additional $90 million in legitimate cash from his nightclubs.

With him was Purly Wyte, a Yonkers female rapper he'd met the prior evening at BB King Blues Club & Grill. She was stunning in a powder blue Valentino dress ($25,000 out of his Chase account), and he was dapper in a Louis Vuitton tuxedo.

Damn Kanye, he was the real Louis Vuitton Don.

They were at LA Bernardin, a French seafood restaurant he'd once dined at with a business associate.

"This some rich nigga shit right here," Purly said.

Cup nodded his head and checked his phone. "Gotta get out of the streets and give back to the streets at the same time. It's always good to experience the better things in life."

As soon as he saw the name Blake on his phone, he answered. "What it look like, King?" he said, hug-ging Purly close up against his side as they strolled together into the restaurant.

"You got Sosa's number?" Blake asked immediately. "Keef?"

"Yeah, nigga. You know who I'm talkin' about. You got his number?"

"You know I got it."

"And you got T-Walk's number too?" "Yeah. Why, what's up?"

"Get 'em all on three way right quick."

"Hold on a second. Just walked in this restaurant. Let me get to my "Yup, I'm waitin'.""

There was already a table for four reserved for Cup and his date.

It took them less than a minute to be led to their table by a cute-faced blonde with lively blue eyes and an abundance of cleavage. All the way to the table, he thought of the situation he was in. He did business with the Black Disciples from 64th and Normal. T-Walk's crew of Gangster Disciples were also big spenders when it came to buying kilos from Cup...kilos that Cup bought from Blake.

He decided not to involve himself in Blake's beef. "I can't do that, Blake," he said as he took his seat.

From across the table, Purly mouthed, "Is that thee Blake? As in Bulletface?"

Cup gave her a brief grin and a nod.

"The fuck do you mean you can't do it?" Blake said. "Them niggas just hit me for ten thousand shirts. Let me know how that drought feel."

Blake hung up without another word.

Cup ordered warm octopus "Carpaccio" in leek compote Peruvian anticucho sauce, staring into Purly's tantalizing brown eyes as she scrunched her face in disgust at his taste for octopus.

He thought of what the robbery meant to his flow of product from Blake as Purly ordered a pan roasted lobster.

It couldn't hurt him much, he decided.

Alexus had to be still pushing tons. He knew the Costilla Cartel much too well. He'd done business with them long before he'd ever met Blake, and he knew that's where the dope was coming from. Blake would be able to get more. Cup was certain of it.

"Oh, my God, you didn't tell me you knew Blake! Do you know Jay Z, too?" Purly was all smiles. "If you could get me on a track with Bulletface that would mean sooooo much to me. I'd be famous overnight." She laughed and traced a fingernail over the tattoo on the index finger of her right hand. "Can you read this? It says Shawn. He's the only reason I wanna be successful, and you know one song with Bulletface would do that."

Cup chuckled. "I'll pay for the verse. He'll do it for you. He's a real nigga like that. I fucks with the li'l homie. We had a few words in the streets, but shit, you know how competitive billionaires can be." He gave her a wink and a grin.

"You ain't no billionaire."

"I really am," he lied. "You just hopped out of a quarter million dollar Bentley that I just bought this morning. I'm rich, biatch." He laughed heartily. "I made a billion before you ever heard of a million. Bullet-face is my li'l nigga. We all billionaires. Welcome to the Billionaire Boys Club."

"Hmm." She poked her lips out and eyed him through thoughtfully cheerful eyes as their food arrived.

"I'm serious," Cup said. "This the money team. We eatin' like kings. Power circle type shit. I can blow a million on you today and not miss it."

"Do it then. Show me. Because I am so worth it." "You are," he agreed, taking a bite of his Carpaccio. "You're sick. How can you eat octopus?"

"Same way I can eat pussy."

"Pussy is way more tasty than octopus," Purly argued. "Hold on a second," Cup said and lifted his smartphone. He called Blake back.

"Yeah, I knew you'd see it my way," Blake said.

"Do me a favor. Get on this song with my li'l buddy Purly Wyte. She the truth, out of Yonkers. You do that and I'll get them niggas on three-way right now."

Purly gasped, wide-eyed.

"Damn, so you gon' blackmail me?" Blake said.

144

"It ain't blackmail. It's business. A favor for a favor." "I'm not trippin'. Just call them niggas."

"Yup. Stay on the line."

King Rio

Chapter 35

"Bae, don't you hear that phone ringing? Want me to answer it?"

Trintino nodded but didn't speak. He put the big blunt he was smoking to his lips and drew in a deep breath of smoke. He coughed twice exhaling; a drop of spittle landed on the chest of his dapper blue Armani suit jacket, which was the same shade of blue as his slacks and silk tie.

They were in the backseat of his dark blue Rolls Royce Ghost, just leaving his six-million-dollar Man-hattan condo. They were on the way to La Bernardin.

His iPhone was resting on the soft white leather seat between them.

Squinting thoughtfully at its screen, he studied Cup's contact photo (Cup sitting on the hood of a black Rolls Royce Phantom) and then picked it up to answer.

"Got Blake on the phone. He wanna holla at you," Cup said.

"I ain't got shit to holla about." T-Walk coughed again, and his face twisted up in anger. He was about to start snapping when Blake cut him off.

"I'm done with this shit, nigga. This shit dumb as fuck. We supposed to be focused on gettin' money! Can't nobody make no bread in the grave! I ain't got shit else to say to you muhfuckas but win. That's it. MBM Gang, nigga. Ain't no hoes over here, and I ain't sayin' no hoes in yo' camp. All I'm sayin' is this shit over. You lost a lotta niggas and I did, too. You war ready and I am, too. We black kings, though. I want my kids to live, nigga! I wanna live to see 'em grow old! I can't do that shit in prison for killin' one of you mothafuckas, and I definitely can't do it from the cemetery. That's all it's gon' be, and I'm not lookin' forward to neither choice, so I say we end this shit now before one of us ain't here no more. Nigga, we grew up in the same city! Now we beefin' like this? I'm done if y'all done. That's for Sosa, too. Cup, text them my number. Anytime somebody got a problem with Blake King, address it to me before the killin' start 'cause y'all know I'm on that and I know y'all on that. One hun'ed."

Blake hung up abruptly.

Stunned by the truth of Blake's words, T-Walk sat there for a moment and said nothing.

The reason he was heading to the French seafood restaurant was to set up the assassination of the same man who'd just squashed the beef.

"I'm about to hang up and call you right back," Cup said. He was back on the line seconds later. "We'll talk when you get here," was all he said before hanging up again.

"What was that about?" Ashley asked immediately. "It was Blake."

"Huh? Why'd he call you?"

"He wanna drop the beef," T-Walk said. "Said we need to focus on gettin' money." He shook his head. "Fuck that. He killed almost every one of my niggas. K.G., Bookie, Craig, Gusto, Li'l Ant, Li'l Regg, the li'l folks in Chicago, Tasia. And that's just what I know he did. How would I look in the streets if I let that shit slide?"

"If it'll stop me from hearing all the shooting that's been going on, I'm with it. Sign me up."

T-Walk's right cheek drew back reluctantly. They'd made it to the restaurant, and the driver— his cousin Aaron — opened his door and waited for them to exit.

In the restaurant, T-Walk instantly spotted Cup at a table in the far back. A blonde waitress ushered him and Ashley to their seats.

No pleasantries were exchanged.

"He wants us to meet up with him in Miami. Said it'll just be him and Alexus," Cup said.

T-Walk asked the girls to excuse themselves for a moment. "I need to use the bathroom anyway," Ashley said.

"Me too, girl." Cup's date got up to leave, and T-Walk found himself gazing at her rotund derriere as she sauntered away with Ashley.

"That's two bad bitches right there," T-Walk commented. Then he got straight to the business at hand. "What we gon' do about this nigga Blake? I got the folks out here wit' me wit' all kinda drums and clips."

"Just chill until we get one more shipment from this nigga. Tell him we need two thousand shirts. Ol' girl gon' do that ASAP for him. I got my half. They'll only charge us ten a shirt. I got $10,000,000, and I know you got it too. Let's grab that shipment and get him out the way right after that. My li'l niggas'll take care of him in Chicago. We can pop bottles in VIP at The Visionary Lounge while they gun his stupid ass down."

T-Walk shook his head. "I really wanna get rid of him right now.

They just whacked Gusto last night. That's big folks. We at that nigga, point blank period. Broad day or whatever. It's on sight."

"Think with your pocket, not out of emotions. Strategize. He just gave up. Let him give up. His name is on fire right now because of all those shootings. His wife got terrorists from overseas pledging to take her life.

Turn to any news channel. All you'll see is ISIS, Alexus, and Blake. Why try to get him when every-body's watching? Especially when we're all out of dope. Let's grab them blocks first, then we can take him out of the game and retire...Well, you ain't gotta retire, but I'm done. I got enough saved up to live good, be rich forever. That's what it's all about anyway, ain't it?"

"You say he wanna meet up in Miami?" T-Walk asked, wondering if the one man he had waiting outside was enough security.

He had left over a dozen more gangsters at his condo, GDs who had left Chicago for New York years earlier, but were still loyal to the mob.

"Yeah, he said he's on his way there on his jet, he wanna meet up to get this shit squashed in person," Cup said. "I say we go along with it."

"I don't know." T-Walk bit his lower lip in thought. "I don't know," he repeated.

"I told him to meet us at King of Diamonds tonight, that way we can all throw money and end the shit like bosses. Back to back Phantoms, you know. Make it look good. Feel me?"

King Rio

T-Walk nodded and ordered lobster for himself and Ashley. He got on his smartphone and made plans for Miami. By the time he was done, the girls were back in their seats and ready to eat.

He remained quiet and listened to their incessant chatter. Evidently, they had a few mutual friends. Purly couldn't believe she was lunching with Ashley "Thunder" Hunter, one of America's hottest reality TV stars and fiancée to the producer of the "Brick House" series himself.

"This nigga Cup knows everybody," Purly said. "I'm eating lobster wit' T-Walk and Thunder. I gotta get a pic of this for Instagram."

"No," T-Walk said, and Cup was shaking his head no. "This lunch never happened. No pictures."

The ladies seemed to understand that it had been something more than a simple lunch; they ate and sipped wine and confabulated about fashion until they were done eating.

Cup called the blonde waitress over and awarded her with a generous $5,000 tip.

Purly Wyte showed her pearly whites in a beaming smile.

Leaving out of La Bernardin, T-Walk was still pondering over whether or not he would send his folks at Blake now or wait for the next dope shipment. Cup walked Purly to his Bentley then joined T-Walk next to the Rolls.

"That terrorist shit crazy, ain't it?" Cup said.

T-Walk eyed his lady's lovely lady lumps as she slipped into the rear of his Ghost. "Those terrorists wouldn't even be over here if it wasn't for Alexus. I'm glad I got out of Georgia last night or else I might've got shot at that airport," he said.

"All we need to do is get some more work outta that bitch before they finally kill her. You see they just killed some people at the MTN Tower in Chicago. That's headquarters for Alexus's TV network, right across the street from the Trump where those suicide bombers tried to get Blake. It's the end of the world for her, but we can still stack a few more millions. Sell them thangs for $30,000 apiece, that's 30 million dollars. Can't lose with that flip."

150

T-Walk stared at Cup for a moment, nodding gently. Not too long ago he and Cup had been at odds over a shooting that was meant to take Blake's life but had ended up wounding Cup's son.

"I'm with it," T-Walk said finally. "One more shipment."

King Rio

Chapter 36

Soothing and melodic, the voice of K. Michelle over a wonderfully constructed beat boomed from Alex-us's pearl white Phantom as it and four more identical Rolls Royces drifted to a stop in front of Casa Casuarina, also known as the Versace Mansion.

The $150,000,000 Miami Beach mansion was owned by Alexus Costilla.

Blake turned off both of his smartphones because they wouldn't stop ringing. He had another show to do, but he wasn't about to do anything until he had his life in order. His first priority was to make sure that his family was safe. Everything else could wait.

His MBM Team had split up at the airport. Mocha was boarding a private jet to Spain, and Blake had sent the others home.

He would need only his wife and her cartel for the plan he had in mind.

"I thought the GDs were after Cup, too?" Alexus said, keeping pace with Blake as they headed inside the mansion. "How'd he get T-Walk on the phone? That seems odd."

"They're up to something," Enrique said from behind them. "I don't trust it."

Blake thought to himself instead of speaking out loud. It was a brief thought.

They don't know what I'm up to.

He smiled and waved hello to attorney Britney Bostic, Dr. Melonie Farr, and— to Blake's surprise — Nona Malden and her brother Biggs.

"Mercedes wanted Biggs here," Britney explained, "and Alexus wanted to talk to Nona."

Blake looked at Alexus with furrowed brows, wondering why she'd sent for a girl he had dated during one of their brief splits.

Alexus gave him a wink. "Go and have a quick session with Dr. Farr. You need it. We both do. I'll have the bank deliver a million or so in ones for tonight at K.O.D. We're trying to figure out what's going on at the MTN Tower in Chicago. And I'm about to call Porsche's black ass. I'll be up to Farr's office right after you."

Blake walked over and shook hands with Biggs, then hugged Britney and Nona before following Mel-onie up to her office while Alexus and the other cartel bosses went to the family room.

He tried to keep his eyes away from Melonie's ass but it looked too good in her asymmetrical red Mar-chesa dress. He knew Marchesa well; he'd purchased dozens of designer dresses for Alexus, and Marchesa was a favorite of hers.

In Dr. Farr's office, Blake went past the leather Versace sofa where Alexus usually relaxed for her ses-sions and stopped at the gold-framed window.

Melonie shook her head in discontent and shut the door as Blake drew a Mac 11 submachine gun from his hip and slipped in a 100-round clip.

"It's sad that it's getting to this," she said. "World War Three is taking place as we speak, all across this country and in other countries, not just Russia and the Middle East. That's why people are buying guns at unprecedented rates. It's crazy, but you need to make sure that you and your family are safe throughout all of it. You're a gangster in the spotlight, like Alexus and her family. I realize that now. The reality of it is frightening. I'm just glad I'll be somewhere with some rich people. If nobody else will survive, Alexus will. She's got this place swarming with bodyguards."

Blake turned to Melonie and grinned. "You're a wise woman."

"Thank you." She sat down behind her desk. "Tell me about the Trump Tower shooting. How did it start?"

"Was in the room with my MBM team, Biggs, Porsche, some strippers, and my bodyguards when I heard the gunshots in the hallway. Then the front wall exploded, killed a few of my bodyguards. We left out and went to the stairwell, headin' downstairs, and that's when a guy stepped out and tried to blow up the bomb vest he was wearing. I shot him down and kept moving. Nothing else to tell you really. It don't bother me."

"What about your recording artist getting killed last night? How is that affecting you?"

He gave her a tight look. "How you think it's affectin' me? That's my nigga. I wanna fuck some shit up."

"But that's not the answer. You do know that, right?"

"The answer is to win. By any means necessary. Did you lock that door?"

"Yes, it's locked. Have a seat. Relax." "I'm good right here."

"There's no need to have a gun drawn in the room with me when Alexus has all those men out there. You remember what happened during that Anderson Cooper inter-view. You're definitely safe around her."

Reluctantly, Blake put the gun in his waistline and went to the sofa.

He hesitated before he sat down.

"I really don't need no therapy." He gazed directly into her pretty brown eyes. "I'm a gangsta. Gangstas don't need therapy. A blunt and some Lean is all I need."

"Do you think it's cool to be a gangster? Because I don't."

Blake felt the growing inclination to look at his smartphone, or the window, or his glistening diamond watch. Anything but, have his brain picked apart by some shrink.

"I'm too deep in the game not to be a gangsta. You know what's goin' down. I'm supplying half of Chi-cago."

"Alexus is supplying half of Chicago," Farr corrected.

"Yeah, but mostly through me," Blake said. "I got niggas buyin' thousands of bricks from me. I'm makin' millions in the dope game and even more in the rap game."

"Yeah, but Alexus is making billions." Farr seemed determined to downplay his situation. She began typing on her desktop computer.

"I know what the fuck my wife makes. I'm just saying—"

"What you're saying is irrelevant. Both of you are wealthy, so I don't want to hear about your money in the streets. All that matters is that your family is safe and that you are safe. Stop thinking like a soldier. Your every move should be for the betterment of your wife and kids. You're a father and a husband now, Blake. Not a street thug. Leave that to the ghetto."

Dr. Farr was making a lot of sense. But what she didn't understand was that the streets were permanently embedded in his mentality. He used to be a goon, was a goon, and always would be a goon. There was no

changing that. Especially with him being a rap star. He was the king of gangsta rap, and there was certain criteria he had to stick to because of it.

"You wouldn't understand my lifestyle," he said. "I'm Bulletface. The real black Scarface. Cocaine to the ceilin'. Choppas like American soldiers wit' drums on them bitches. These niggas just hatin' extra hard 'cause I'm ballin' extra hard. I'm ready, though." He chuckled once. "And they don't even know it."

Melonie eased back in her white leather Versace swivel chair. She was the epitome of beautiful, a redbone with curves and genuine pulchritude. She wore a host of diamonds on her wrists, ears, neck, and fingers— the signature of all female associates of the Costilla Cartel— yet she still managed a look of elegance.

"You gon' be my Olivia Pope one day," Blake said suddenly. He grinned, shocked at himself for saying it, but not at all regretting it.

Melonie's eyes brightened. The skin on her forehead rose. Her jaw dropped into a half-open smile.

"You did not just say that."

Blake laughed. "Just fuckin' witchoo." "No, you weren't. I'm telling Alexus."

"I thought this kinda shit was confidential? I'll sue you." Melonie's sweet smile broadened.

Then a sudden roar of high-caliber gunfire from somewhere outside the mansion froze them in place.

Blake drew his Mac 11, got up, and headed for the door.

"America has become as evil as Iraq, Syria, and Mexico," Farr said as Blake snatched open the door and stormed out into the hallway.

Chapter 37

Alexus gasped at the barrage of gunfire and spilled half of her Ace of Spades champagne in the haste to put the crystal stem glass on the coffee table in front of her.

Instinctively, she dug in her Birkin and clamped a hand around the handle of her .50-caliber Desert Ea-gle. Enrique raised a gold-plated AK-47 from the floor next to his easy chair and went to his phone to find out what was going on. Biggs, who'd been able to bring his guns along on the jet Alexus had sent for him, pulled a Mac 11 from his Louis Vuitton duffle bag. Thirty heavily armed Costilla Cartel bodyguards with concealed firearms became thirty men with their guns drawn. Flako and Pedro drew their own golden Eagles with heavy 50-round drums magazines.

The Costilla Cartel was the definition of war ready.

"It's a group of Hatians, we believe," Enrique said. "About twenty of them. Four blocks down from here they're in a gunfight with our men."

"Call Rick Ross and ask him what the fuck is going on!" Alexus shouted, because it was her first thought.

She quickly changed her tone and said what she knew her father would have said.

"Kill them all!"

Blake ran into the room with his submachine gun in hand. "Haitians," Alexus explained.

"Hatians?" Blake asked

"Yeah," Enrique repeated. "Twenty of them, attacking our men. Get your people on a fucking leash."

Blake scowled. "The fuck was that supposed to mean?" Enrique waved him off and went back to talking into his phone.

Alexus walked over to Blake and wrapped her arms around him.

She pressed her face in the crook of his neck and clung to him as the gunfire continued.

"We good, baby," he said, kissing her forehead. "Enrique, that shit almost sounded racist. I beat up Mex-icans too, nigga."

"You know he didn't mean it that way," Alexus said.

Enrique barked, "An SUV just broke through our first line of defense. We need to get out of here."

Police sirens screamed in the distance. But then there was the sound of screeching tires and a harsh me-tallic crash, and the sirens stopped.

The gunfire went on.

Alexus peeled away from Blake and rushed back to the table to pick up her iPad. She went to the man-sion's camera surveillance system and studied their immediate surroundings.

"No need to look there," Enrique said. "We're all clear to go. Let's head to the island like we should have done in the first place."

No one questioned Enrique's orders, but Blake regarded his wife's head of security with a stringent stare as they hustled out of the mansion toward their waiting Rolls-Royces. They were stopped in their tracks by the sight of bullets skewering through the first layers of the bullet-resistant windows on their sparkling white Phantoms.

The gunfight four blocks down the street was moving closer. Alexus cuddled up close beside Blake, staring vacantly at her gold-plated handgun as her security team moved forward in military formation and sprayed their MP-5 submachine guns in the direction of the incoming rounds.

"We'll take the Sprinter," Enrique said, grabbing Alexus by the wrist and sprinting off to the side of the mansion.

She stumbled in her five-inch Louboutins along the way but managed to keep her balance. There was a bodyguard already waiting at the Mercedes Sprinter van with the engine running and the side door open, and a dozen others were pulling up in cocaine-white Tahoes and Suburbans.

Alexus's men were suddenly everywhere.

More sirens blared in the distance, and the gunfight continued.

Alexus sat on Blake's lap in his usual seat at the door. Nona sat on her brother's lap. Attorney Bostic ended up on Dr. Farr's lap to make room for Flako, Pedro, and Enrique.

The Sprinter's tires burned rubber as it raced off.

"This isn't how I intended for my day to go," Alexus said.

"Why did you bring Nona out here?" Blake asked her in a whisper.

"We'll talk about that later."

"I'm never coming back to this mansion again. Every time I'm here something goes down."

"I was thinking that, too." Alexus turned to gaze out her window and got a glimpse of her men battling the Hatians in the middle of Collins Avenue as her Mercedes van raced down 11th Street. "It's either T-Walk or Chief Keef who sent them, and I'm guessing Keef. He has ties to the Zoe Pound. That's why I said call Ross. He'll know what all this is about."

Blake palmed his forehead and gave it a squeeze. He pulled Alexus tight against his chest and kissed the side of her neck.

"I wish I could just meet up with both of them and shoot it out. That would end all this drama," he said thoughtfully.

Biggs patted a hand on Blake's shoulder." I know we just met, but I'm wit' the shits, bruh. For real for real. Just gimme the word and I'm blowin'. You put me on my feet my first day out the feds. I owe you."

"You don't owe me nothin'," Blake said.

"What does 'wit' the shits' mean?" Alexus asked.

Nona said, "It means you're dumb enough to shoot at anybody."

This brought a nervous laugh out of Alexus. They were getting away safely. Police cars and SUVs were speeding past in the opposite lane.

"If we live through all this mess that's going on," Alexus said, turning to Blake, "I'm done. We can retire with $150 billion. No more drug dealing for me and no more rap for you. Let these niggas kill each other all they want. As long as we're safe I'm good."

King Rio

Chapter 38

"Fuck goin' to the airport," Blake said. He opened his wife's Birkin bag and began searching for her stash of loud. "Go to the car lot. Let me buy somethin' new to pop up in at the club. I got a meetin' at K.O.D tonight. Can't miss it."

Alexus squinted at him.

"I want a car, too," Nona said. "Y'all really owe me a car anyway after what happened last time I ran into yo' uncle, Alexus." She rolled her eyes at Flako, who had sent a bullet at her at Blake's Highland Park mansion, deeply grazing the side of her head.

Biggs frowned. "What happened?"

"Nothin'," Nona said quickly and smiled her perfect smile. She was flawless in a white and yellow striped mini-dress and peep-toe Gucci heels. Her impeccable pie-shaped face had just enough makeup.

Alexus caught Blake staring at Nona; she put her fingertips on his forehead, and shoved his head into the headrest.

He smiled.

"Cars for everybody today," he said, still cheesing. "I'm feelin' generous."

"I bet you are." Alexus wasn't smiling, and again Blake wondered why she had Nona there in the first place.

Enrique ordered the driver to detour to Sanfer Sports Cars on 51st Street in Miami. As they were passing through Little Haiti, Blake kept his eyes on the streets, smoking a thick cigarillo full of Kush, and ignoring the urge to turn his phones on. Britney opened a window and complained about the smoke. Alexus laughed and hit the blunt twice herself before handing it back to Blake.

At the car dealership, Blake leapt out and fell in love with a blood- red 2015 Porsche 918 Spyder con-vertible that cost a whopping $929,000. He wasted no time buying it, along with a red 2015 Ferrari 458 Italia for Biggs ($265,000), a cherry red 2014 Ferrari California for Nona ($205,000), a shiny white 2015 Lamborghini Huracan for Dr. Farr ($317,000), and a matte-black

2015 Lamborghini Aventador for Britney ($440,000). The final bill, charged to his American Express black card, was over $2.1 million.

Although Alexus and the other Costillas could have purchased the entire car dealership, they were con-tent sitting in the Sprinter while Blake and the others signed the paperwork for their cars and walked out with their keys and titles.

Blake helped Alexus out of the van to speak alone with her.

"Go to the island with the kids," he said. "I'm just gon' talk to this nigga T-Walk, get this shit squashed."

"Who are you lying to? Am I supposed to believe that?" Alexus grabbed her hips. "You're going to start shooting. I know you like the back of my hand. I'm coming with you"

"No, you're not." "Hmm."

"I'll be straight to the island, bae. I promise. Let me just talk to these niggas myself."

"Those Hatians weren't talking. I'm not letting you go alone. If you're going, I'm sending the full security team with you."

"I'm cool with that. Just make sure you got the kids and your mom safe on the island. I'm takin' Biggs with me."

"When will you be flying in?"

"Right afterwards. I promise. I might throw a few bands at the club, but then I'm out."

Alexus regarded him with a stern expression. He put his hands on her ass and kneaded the meaty cheeks as he leaned forward and molded his lips to hers.

She pulled her head back.

"That kissing and squeezing doesn't always work," she claimed, but already her expression had softened and she was creeping forward for another smooch. "I just talked to Porsche. She swears up and down she didn't drug you. She said she was drinking some Molly water or something and you might have accidentally grabbed that, but it couldn't have been anything else."

"I ain't trippin'. Long as I'm alive, baby. That's the only thing that matters." He turned to admire his sleek new Porsche. Biggs was parked in front of it, sitting behind the wheel of his Ferrari, revving the engine, and

162

smiling wickedly, and the others were lined up at the parking lot exit ready to leave with Alexus.

"That was so nice of you. Getting them those cars." Alexus pecked her lips on the tip of his nose. "Be safe. I'll see you later."

She tried slipping out of Blake's arms, but his strong hands wouldn't unleash the grip on her bountiful buttocks. His dick grew hard in his Versace boxer-briefs. It seemed to be thinking for his hands.

"Go, boy." Alexus gave him a gentle slap on the cheek and bit down on the center of her bottom lip. Her voice was as soft as cotton. "You'll get the goodies later. Don't be too late coming in. You better be on that island by midnight. And I mean on the dot."

"I'll be there," Blake said.

Reluctantly, he let go of her pillowy derrière and gave her one last kiss while a few of the bodyguards loaded his duffle bags into the Spyder.

He got himself together; fixed a cup of Promethazine with Codeine and Sprite on ice from the Sprinter's refrigerator; rolled another cigarillo of Kush; snapped a few pics of his and Biggs's new toys for Instagram, and pulled off ahead of Biggs with the Mac 11 on his lap.

When he checked his rearview mirror, five white Tahoes full of Costilla Cartel militants were following close behind him.

King Rio

Chapter 39

You ain't never met a nigga like Blake, J's on in that foreign thang Bad Asian bitch gimme foreign brain, Chinese K's they foreign bang Real nigga and you're a lame, drama come I resort to bangin'

Got resorts and islands from corporate grindin', and I'm still hood I ain't never changin'

Dick long like a ruler, clips long as two rulers

Yo' bitch bad I might do her; you walk in get blammed wit this Ruger Money Bagz Gang, she gon' choose us, and ain't nann nigga gon shoot us.

Don't fuck around wit' my shootas, li'l niggas wit the shits they'll do ya.

I'm freestylin' like Hoova, I mean Hova, a new schoola

Nigga I'm the king of this whole game, it'll NEVER be a new ruler Say hello to da bad guy, young Bullet-face I'ma bad guy

Mac on me wit' a hun'ed in it, I'll let it shout like a mad guy

Roll up some loud and get mad high

MBM we mad fly, soon's the jet lands head to dem bands wit dat yoppa on me— Bad guy...

The Spyder's sound system was bumping "Bad Guy," another track off Bulletface's "Took the Throne" album, when he pulled up to King of Diamonds on 5th Avenue.

It was 7 o'clock p.m. Eastern Time, and already the strip club was jam-packed. Throngs of scantily clad young women and men in their very best outfits and jewels were bunched together in a line that stretched for two blocks. Blake had made a few calls to his celebrity friends, and many of them were just arriving. Floyd "Money" Mayweather's white Bugatti and Birdman's white Maybach Landaulet were pulling in. Nicki Minaj was climbing out of a pink Lamborghini. Yo Gotti was walking in with Ross, Trina, 2 Chainz, Boosie, Meek Mill, and Gunplay. Big Sean and Ariana Grande stepped out of a Bentley just as Blake was getting out of the Porsche.

"Bulletface, I love you!" a girl in line shouted. She was dark and pretty, slender, with a gold tooth and ample curves. Her friends and a number of other girls were also screaming proclamations of love to him and the rest of their celebrity crushes.

Blake's eyes fell upon a Carolina blue Aston Martin and a black Range Rover Evoque that a crowd of women was crowded around. They were a few car-lengths ahead of him. Two mulatto-skinned men in expensive-looking business suits were getting out of the Rover.

T-Walk and Cup.

Blake wasn't surprised to see Chief Keef and his dread-headed minions—Tadoe and Capo— emerge from the Aston in custom Glo Gang apparel.

Blake stood at his driver's side door, lit a blunt, and sipped a mouthful of Lean as the cartel bodyguards encircled him and a flock of club-goers started toward him. Biggs appeared at his side with both their duffle bags, and together they headed into the club.

Blake's bling— worth $5 million altogether — crushed everyone else's by a landslide, and no one let him forget it. He received a hundred jewelry related compliments within minutes of entering the club, and soon thereafter, he was throwing thousands of singles at the beautiful nude dancers. He ended up standing between Floyd and Baby, with the other rappers close behind them. Just about, everyone who was anyone, surrounded him. He ordered 500 bottles of Armand de Brignac and passed them out gratuitously.

T-Walk and Cup were far to the left of Blake's table. Three tables away, to be exact. Cup excused himself from T-Walk's presence and approached Blake.

"What it is, Li'l Lord," Cup said, biting a cigar in the corner of his mouth and wielding a bottle of Ciroc. "He say dat shit dead, li'l homie.

Finito. Sosa on the same shit. Live yo' muhfuckin' life. We wanna see you shine, see you win. MBM like MMG now. Get money, li'l bruh. Shit, we want two thousand shirts if anything. Get on some racks. That's all I'm talkin'.""

Half the club was watching. They saw T-Walk. They saw Chief Keef and his GBE gang. But most of all they saw Bulletface, the young black man who was handsome and heavily bejeweled and worth billions, the youthful king of Hip Hop who was known to squeeze the trigger every now and then.

He gave a nod. "Tell 'em it's over then."

Each of the two large Louis Vuitton duffle bags at his feet contained

$1,000,000 in bank-new hundred-dollar bills. He opened one and took out ten $10,000 packets, since his $75,000 in ones was already on the floor around the pole Blac Chyna was twerking on a few feet in front of him.

Cup sent a text message, and seconds later T-Walk and Chief Keef were at Blake's table.

He kept his eyes on both of them. Everyone did.

"What up, nigga." T-Walk reached out for a handshake. Blake hesitated. "We good?"

"Over," T-Walk said. "Salute to the whole MBM team. R.I.P. dem guys, free dem guys, you feel me?"

With a modicum of reluctance, Blake shook T-Walk's hand. "Stay the fuck away from my bitch and my shorties and we good. I'll talk to her about gettin' you back in with MTN. Get them real millions back up."

The tension had been palpable moments earlier; now the whole club seemed to relax. Blake threw a few more thousands at the big-bootied model and sipped from his cup of Lean. Rick Ross passed him a massive blunt of loud and he sucked in a lungful.

Chief Keef muttered something incoherent to Blake. Sounded like, "Dat shit ain't on shit, man, but niggas wit the shits keep dem poles on at all times...we ain't hit no stangs doe don't know who robbed dem spots...we gotta get in the studio...shit over, man, my Zoes wasn't thinkin'...Three hun'ed GBE shit MBM shit..."

Blake took that to mean Sosa had probably sent the Hatians, or maybe they'd come on his behalf. One or the other. You never knew with Chief Keef.

"We gotta stop tryna kill each other and get this money," Blake said. "If it ain't good don't say it type shit. Get in that studio and write. Record.

Drop albums. Do shows. Thumb through checks. That's all it should be
about. All this drama shit with you"—he pointed at T-Walk — "started when yo' niggas robbed me the day I met Alexus. Today that shit ends. Let's be rich forever like the fat homie Rozay. Be kings and live long. I'm the connect, nigga. I'm the king of all kings but God. If y'all wanna get money wit' me let's get it."

"We can start wit' the two thousand shirts," T-Walk said. "I got my $10 million. I know Cup got it, too."

They exchanged numbers and Yo Gotti and Floyd commented on how it was a good look seeing Bullet-face at peace with his longtime enemies.

"The Money Team," Floyd said. "Get money and be the richest and the best at everything you do. You're the best rapper; I'm the best fighter..."

Blake tuned Floyd out and instead turned his attention to T-Walk, who was talking to Jim Jones and Juelz Santana a few feet away. He tried to decide if selling 2,000 kilos of cocaine to Cup and T-Walk was a wise idea given the unfortunate circumstances surrounding him and Alexus.

A quick $20 million didn't sound too bad, though. Blake knew that one phone call from Alexus was all it took to have the kilos delivered. Why not? he thought.

He threw over $200,000 in hundreds at Chyna, and she deserved every big-faced Benjamin. Her twerk-ing skills were unmatched. She bounced her ass and popped her pussy, sometimes upside down and sometimes right side up, never taking her eyes off Bulletface.

Biggs was making it rain on another stripper to Chyna's left as a Bulletface track boomed throughout the club, and a lot of the women were trying to figure out who he was.

"I'll get those shirts to you. Let's get this guap." Blake extended his double Styrofoam of Lean for a toast. T-Walk, Chief Keef, and the other African American moguls extended their bottles and Styrofoams.

Floyd leaned toward Blake. "From champ to champ, be careful," he said quickly.

Instead of responding to Floyd's wary advice, Blake hefted another pile of hundreds out of his bag to entertain his favorite dancer.

Throwing Benjamins seemed to be the trick to getting everyone's attention in a strip club. Blake had known it for years now. He'd probably

blown a good $30 million at strip clubs all across the country since becoming a rap superstar.

He fanned through a $10,000 packet of crisp hundreds in seconds and started on the next.

"You see how I thumb through these bands, Chyna?" he asked, studying her radiant smile as she, on her hands and knees, looked over her shoulder at him and twerked her massive gelatinous derrière in his direction.

He ripped off the bank wrapper on another packet and showered Blac Chyna with the whole $10,000.

It was then that he decided the drama with T-Walk and Sosa wasn't worth the casualties. People were taking pictures and TMZ would more than likely be reporting on the squashed beefs. Maybe peace could prevail.

Blake was bone-tired of war.

He refilled his cup and drank and smoked and made it rain until he'd emptied his duffle of the entire $1 million.

At the bottom of the bag lay two Mac-11s with 100-round clips. Blake saw T-Walk's eyes on the guns as he zipped the duffle shut. He took a bunch of pictures with the rich rap stars and some

Bulletface fans and purchased another 200 bottles of Ace of Spades. He left

K.O.D shortly thereafter, relieved that all the beef had finally come to an end.

For the moment, at least.

King Rio

Chapter 40

Blake was glad to finally get away from everybody. Alone in the Spyder, he rolled another blunt and refilled his double-stacked Styrofoam for the fourth time. He got on I-95 leaving K.O.D and pushed the Porsche to 145 miles per hour. Biggs had no trouble keeping up in his Ferrari. The two sports cars veered around the other vehicles as if they were obstacles on a driving course.

"Ferrari Gang," yet another track off Bulletface's "Took the Throne" album was bumping from the Spyder's speakers.

Ferrari gang in the fast lane, duffle bags big cash lane

Up the strap let it blam bang, 'cause these fuck niggas so damn lame And mah li'l niggas so damn gang...Vice Lord, VL's up

We ride around wit' a thousand rounds, nigga diss me and get shelled up

The streets nowadays hell, bruh, my niggas gone, all murda cases I ain't the only nigga walkin' up dat you can give the nickname Bulletface

Gold bottles, full o' Ace...LA mansions, full o' safes

Semi-trailers, full o' crates...got Kush and yay, what you tryna pay? Got shooters benched like D. Rose and they dyin' to play

Pull up in that black 'Rari, it's a movie shoot call Lionsgate

I bought a couple 458s, Got twenty 'Raris in twenty states

Young street nigga, Bill Gates money, G5 or better don't try to hate Queen A come fly wit' me...I bet I beat it up mightily

And I'm solid Trav, an Almighty T, that's the way it is how it gotta be Keep it real witchoo so don't lie to me, we can stack the billions up nightily

I mean nightly, fuckin' up words off this iced Lean in my white T I'm so icy, like I'm Gucci; call me Louis Mane or young Bruce Lee That Italia go about two hun'ed, cop get behind me gon' lose me And I'll whip up in a different 'Rari dat same night wit' dem guys wit' me

Simba shit, I got lions wit me, they ride wit' me and they'll die wit' me..

The four white Tahoes full of Costilla Cartel security got left far behind on the highway. Blake dialed Biggs's number and told him they were heading to the docks where Alexus's private mega yacht — her father had named it The Omnipotent — was waiting. It had been shipped to the coast of Miami for the sole purpose of transporting the family to and from the private island.

"Man, how the fuck did y'all get so much money?" Biggs asked. "Can't believe you got me a muhfuckin Ferrari. Never in my life thought I'd be able to drive somethin' like this."

"This is just the beginning," Blake said, his voice cracking because his lungs were full of Kush smoke. "We gon' ball till the wheels fall off, bruh. When Li'l Lord comes home, he'll get the same kinda blessings you got. This that real mob shit. We gon' run the game like Al Capone did in the 1920s, and we'll Valentine's Day massacre some niggas if need be."

"On Chief," Biggs said. "What's the thought on them opps, though?

T-Walk and Chief Keef."

Blake glanced at his watch. "I'll get money wit' the nigga T-Walk.

Fuck that war shit. I'll be in prison forever fuckin' around wit' these niggas. I'm tryna be rich forever, not locked up forever."

"I feel you but damn you can't just let it slide like that. I'll handle that shit if anything."

"I'll let that beef simmer for now. No need to rush. They gon' get what's comin' to 'em, but it's gon' be on my time." Blake coughed about a dozen times from one inhalation of smoke. He put the blunt out and slaked his thirst with some Lean. "All we on for now is this money. You wit' me?"

"What kinda question is that? You know I'm wit' it. I'm fresh out the feds, still got all the connect's info. I can sit back and let my young niggas trap all day for me. I'm already 'bout to go to the store. Gotta feed the block. Niggas out there starvin'. Gotta get some guns, too."

"Don't worry about nothin'. Just give me the address and tell the brothas to wait for some Mexicans to show up. They'll get that shit today." Blake thought of the robberies at his stash houses and gritted his teeth in anger. He'd had over 5,000 kilos of uncut cocaine left at his suburban stash houses. "I gotta find out who took my spots down. Fufu ass niggas gon' get laid down about that. Meach said it was GBE."

"Like I said, just gimme the word."

Blake nodded and grinned, admiring his reflection in the rearview mirror. His diamond-encrusted teeth were sparkling. He and Biggs were neck and neck on the interstate, zipping past Little Haiti.

"You ever been here before today?" he asked Biggs. "Florida, I mean."

"Nah, but I been to ten fed joints in nine different states. You know how they ship niggas around in the feds."

"I'ma get you a condo out here, and a million in legit money put in an account for you. Keep it as a vaca-tion spot, you know. Somewhere to get away. You need it after that bid. Bring some bad bitches through and show 'em this shit real."

"I want your wife's sister. She bad and thick as fuck. Alexus say she the reason I'm here. Said she want a nigga."

"Yeah, she married to another one of the Lords but he locked up, got some murders. She need a new nigga."

Biggs paused; then, "I got out and got blessed. Met the richest nigga in the game. Li'l Lord always told me you was a real muhfucka."

"You only live once. Can't take none of this money to the grave wit' me. Might as well bless the real nig-gas I cross paths wit'. It'll come back tenfold. Blessings always come back around to those who give 'em."

"Well, I'm glad I got picked for the blessings," Biggs said with a laugh.

Alexus rang in on Blake's other line. He told Biggs he'd call back and switched over.

"Hey, babyyyy!" Alexus chimed over a cacophony of loud music and elated feminine screams of "WOOOO!"

He heard Porsche say, "Girl, he got a Mandingo!" Blake frowned.

"The fuck is goin' on over there?" he asked.

Chapter 41

Alexus laughed, knowing for certain that Blake would not be pleased to know what his wife was up to. She had just escaped to a bathroom down the hall from the family room where the real action was taking place.

There were eight Herculean male strippers in the family room, along with an array of sex toys, penis-shaped treats, and enough liquor to get everyone fully inebriated.

Since she was pregnant, Alexus stuck to red wine, but that didn't stop her from enjoying the festivities. She'd already had several lap dances. One such encounter resulted in her being lifted up onto a brawny dark- skinned man's shoulders.

She looked at her makeup in the sink mirror, and then smiled at herself.

"We're having that little party I told you about," she said into the phone, trying to make the bachelorette party seem a lot less spectacular than it actually was. "Porsche sent for some Miami entertainers. Everybody's drinking. You know, girl stuff."

"What kinda girl stuff?" Blake asked.

"Just...you know. Girl stuff." She gave her reflection a conspiratorial smirk. "You can stay out tonight if you want to. I ain't trippin'. Just be safe."

"You know you got me fucked up."

She giggled innocently. "What? I haven't done anything."

"A'ight."

"What do you have an attitude about? You're the one who did it first.

It's my turn to party now."

"Don't make me fuck you up, Alexus."

"It's no fun when the rabbit has the gun, is it? You can feel how I felt that night you had Maliah all on you."

Alexus wondered if a wave of jealousy had washed over Blake as he envisioned her fucking the strip-pers. Of course, she never would betray her sacred marital vows, but the idea of him thinking otherwise excited her.

"Let's FaceTime," she said, turning her back to the mirror and eyeing her meaty derrière; tucked under-neath her snug white Chanel dress, it looked amazing. Almost like a mirror shot of Cubana Lust. Only the 10- carat white diamonds in Alexus's Chanel necklace, tennis bracelet, and earrings. There was no doubt to her immense wealth and beauty.

Blake hung up and was on FaceTime seconds later, squinting at her, and meticulously studying the back-ground. "You in the bathroom?"

"Duh." She rolled her eyes. "Don't go back out there."

"Are you crazy? I'm having a great time. Please don't kill my vibe." She smirked again.

"I'll vibe yo' ass to the hospital," Blake said, and he sounded serious.

His expression was tight and stern. His eyes were fixed on hers. "Boy, please. Go out and have fun. I'll call you later."

Alexus ended the call without waiting for a reply. She was in too much of a hurry to get back to the celebration.

Chapter 42

Grinding his teeth together jealously, Blake veered off the highway and led Biggs and the security team to his twenty-million-dollar Miami mansion.

Shay, a skinny brown girl he'd known for years, resided at the mansion with Lakita "Bubbles" Thomas, a big-bootied stripper who'd been Blake's girlfriend for a brief while some years back.

The two sexy women were waiting in the driveway when Blake pulled up. He got out with his duffle and waved for Biggs to follow him into the mansion.

"Damn," Kita said. "I can't even get a hi, a hello, nothin'?" She was on Blake's heels.

"This my muhfuckin' house. Fuck I need to say hi for?" Blake said. He'd given Kita and Shay $500,000 cash for setting someone up for him a few weeks earlier, and judging from their expensive dresses, heels, and jewelry, they'd probably spent most of it already.

"You need to start calling me sometimes," Kita persisted, walking alongside him. "I heard what happened at K.O.D. They say you, T-Walk, and Chief Keef cool now."

"How the fuck you find that out?"

"Twitter. You know everything on Twitter." "Yo' ass just nosey."

"Boy, ain't nobody thinking about you. I saw it like everybody else saw it. TMZ just tweeted about it."

Thoroughly angered by Alexus's party, Blake went straight to the poolside bar and poured himself a shot of Patrón, ignoring Kita as she put her hands on her hips and smiled at him.

Biggs and Shay began to converse on the terrace behind the extravagant mansion. Blake swallowed his drink in one gulp and poured another.

"What's wrong with you?" Kita murmured. "Nothin'."

"Something is definitely wrong. I thought you quit drinking."

"Left my Lean in the car."

"Want me to go and get it?"

Blake shook his head no and set his mouth on fire with the second shot of tequila. He clenched his teeth tightly together. His left hand was a balled fist. He tried not to let the jealous feelings overwhelm him, but they did anyway. The idea of other men touching on his wife infuriated him to no end.

"Tell me what's wrong," Kita said. She sat on the stool beside him and poured herself a shot.

"It ain't shit," he said. "Alexus havin' a bachelorette party, and I don't like her bein' around no male strip-pers. I know how Chyna and Maliah was on me." He paused. "She bet' not fuck none of them niggas."

Kita laughed.

"Ain't shit funny," Blake said.

"It is funny. You niggas always wanna give up some dick but go crazy if you think a nigga wanna fuck your girls. That's called bein' a hypocrite."

Blake turned to Kita and grinned. He noticed Biggs and Shay were a little closer to each other than they'd been before on the patio. He put a hand on Kita's hand and gave it a soft squeeze.

"I miss yo' thick ass," he said. "Yeah right. You don't miss me."

"Yes I do. Remember how we used to fuck all the time? I miss that shit too."

"I just bet you do." "I do."

An amused expression arose on Kita's cute caramel face. The snug- fitting black dress she wore made Blake's mouth water. He dropped a hand to her thigh and rubbed, gazing into her eyes. She shook her head.

"You're a mess, Blake. You really are."

No resistance meant further exploration for Blake's wandering hand; it moved to her inner thigh and up under the short dress. Smoothly shaven pussy met his fingertips and he massaged her roughly.

She bit the center of her lower lip and inhaled sharply. Momentarily, her eyes rolled up in their sockets. The fact that Kita's ass was nearly as large and perfectly round as Alexus's made his dick hard immediately. "Boy, you gon' make me get reeeeal nasty in a minute," she said. Out of the corner of his eye, Blake saw Shay ease forward and kiss Biggs.

He said fuck it and did the same to Kita. It was meant to be a simple kiss on the lips, just to let her know that he meant business, but she bit his bottom lip and sucked on it as his middle finger slid into her lubricious pussy and wriggled fiercely.

She moaned and released her oral hold on his lip.

"You know what I miss?" she said, finding his erection through his pants and rubbing it. "I told Shay about this big ass dick and she ain't believe me. Pull it out."

Blake didn't hesitate. He stood up and pulled it out right in front of her. Her eyes went wide as if it was her first time seeing his foot-long love muscle. She stroked it in both hands and then squatted down before him.

Shay walked over and watched as Kita put her lips around the long black pole and moved forward until most of it was lodged in her throat. She kept it buried there for a moment, bobbing gently. Her throat made squishy noises. He grabbed her head and fucked her mouth until she her eyes got watery and she pulled back.

"Get it, girl," Shay encouraged.

Chuckling and displaying his signature diamond grin, he put his hands on her head and guided his sali-va-coated phallus back into the warm depths of her throat.

She slurped and sucked him so good his toes curled in his expensive sneakers.

Shay grabbed Biggs's hand and preceded him into the mansion, leaving Blake alone with Kita. He picked his smartphone up and checked it to see if Alexus had messaged him.

She hadn't.

Just about everyone else had called or messaged him, but not Alexus.

He leaned back on the stool and poured himself a third shot. It played like a flamethrower going down. His face twisted and tensed.

He grabbed the thirty-thousand-dollar bundle of hundreds that was hanging out in his right pocket and put it on the bar.

"That's all you," he said, and pulled his dick out from between her greedily slurping lips. He rubbed and slapped the bulbous head on her tongue as it flickered sporadically. His grin stretched when she went back to sucking him. "That's that shit I like right there. Keep suckin' it like that. Put it in that throat."

She took him to the rear of her throat and continued to push forward, trying to get the rest of his thick length in her mouth.

A few minutes of that was almost too much for Blake. He pulled back again. Getting up, Kita showed a seductive smile. She went to her big Louis Vuitton bag and returned with a Magnum condom. Blake slapped a hand onto her huge derrière and watched it vibrate under the dress.

She sauntered over to a black leather chaise lounge next to the pool, and Blake followed, stroking his erection and leering at her beautiful curves as if they were his prey. In a way, that's exactly what her curves were at the moment. He was a lion and her pussy was a zebra.

She kneeled on the chaise lounge, face down, ass up, and he hooked his thumbs under her dress and pushed it up to the middle of her back.

The sight was so indelible that he was tempted to take a picture. He put on the condom and hurriedly slipped inside her...

Chapter 43

Chopper, a dark-skinned man of about 6'2" with bulging muscles and long dreadlocks, was grinding in Alexus's face to August Alsina's "Kissin' on My Tattoos," and she loved every minute of it...that was until Porsche reached in between them and unsheathed his incredibly long sausage from the black thong under-wear he was wearing.

Alexus gasped.

Porsche guided the head of his dick into Alexus's open mouth, but Alexus quickly shoved him back and frowned.

"Y'all got me fucked up," Alexus said. She instantly caught an attitude.

The other girls— Mercedes, Porsche, Britney, Melonie, and Nona— were all seated on the comfy white Italian leather U-shaped sofa with Alexus, throwing hundreds of hundred-dollar bills from her Chanel suitcase at the eight muscled men and drinking from bottles of Ace.

Alexus had a glass of red wine. It was her third glass.

"Don't be so scared, girl," Porsche said, still stroking Chopper's enormous pole.

She pulled it to her mouth and began fellating him. Alexus cracked up laughing. "Uuuugh. You are so trifle." "Ain't that the truth," Melonie said.

Porsche stopped sucking the stranger and jacked him on her tongue. Mercedes, Nona, and Britney cheered merrily.

"Alexus, that's what you need to be doing," Nona said. "Shit, the way Blake was turnin' up at his bache-lor party, I'm surprised you ain't butt naked right now."

Alexus's brows moved close together, as she turned to look at Nona. "What's that supposed to mean?"

"It means what it sounds like. I was there. He turned all the way up."

Britney waved off the conversation. "Let whatever happened at his party stay there, just like whatever we do stays here."

"Straight up, though," Nona agreed. "You can't name a bitch hotter than Alexus. You like the new Be-yoncé, just with that Oprah dough."

"Oprah?" Melonie scoffed. "Oprah would die to have Alexus's bank accounts."

"Let me show y'all how it's done," Mercedes said as she unsheathed another stripper's not-so-long phal-lus and sucked it into her mouth.

Alexus couldn't believe it. The remaining men were looking at the women like a fat kid looks at a box of Twinkies.

She kept her cool and sipped her wine. The pile of bills left in her hand would not be thrown because everybody had her fucked up. She wasn't about to cheat on Blake. Not now, not ever.

Britney's smartphone rang just then, and she jumped up yelling, "Alexus! Your surprise is here!" She rushed out of the room and returned seconds later with a ninth male stripper.

It was a friend of her mother's boyfriend's nicknamed Manchild. Blake had broken his jaw at the Versace Mansion a while back, but

Alexus had had a crush on Manchild ever since she first laid eyes on him that day.

She was puzzled by his stripper getup— a black thong, a large brimmed black hat, and Timberland boots.

"I ordered you a personal dancer," Britney said, pulling Alexus to her feet.

"Boy...Blake is going to kill us," Alexus murmured.

Britney waved off the comment and led Alexus and Manchild to a bedroom down the hall. She shoved Alexus through the door and pulled it shut the door.

Chapter 44

Neal Miller had on numerous occasions been mistaken for Morgan Freeman. In fact, years ago when he was still a homicide detective in Michigan City, Indiana, he'd arrested Blake King and listened to the now- billionaire call him a number of names, including a "Morgan Freeman lookin' muhfucka."

So he wasn't at all surprised when he walked in Rita Mae Bishop's master bedroom and got called that very same name.

"Well, look at my Morgan," she said, setting her Bible aside and sitting up in bed.

He kicked off his shoes and left his suitcase at the door. "We just flew in. I brought Pat. Think he's downstairs with Alexus."

"Pat?"

"The guy Blake punched at the Miami Beach mansion." "Oh." Rita nodded. "Manchild."

Stepping around to the vacant side of the bed, Neal said, "I got something to show you."

"Oh Lord." Rita never liked when Neal had news. It was never good news, always some unfortunate event that could have come straight from the pages of a James Patterson novel.

Neal got in bed and slipped beneath the covers. "God, I'm tired. Getting old," he said.

"What's the news?" Rita said. "And please don't tell me my daughter or her husband are under investiga-tion again, because today is not the day."

Neal smiled. "Fine. I won't tell you." Rita sighed.

Neal gave her a tight hug and a kiss on the cheek. "It's not what you think," he said. "It's just...Well, you know the country's on high alert after today's terrorist attacks. No one ever thought ISIS would be targeting the richest couple in America, but clearly, they are. We can't afford to overlook that."

"Get to the point."

Another smile. "I believe I know what they want, what'll end all the attacks. And I believe Alexus can give it to them."

"Yeah? And what's that?"

"When Jenny murdered your brother and his family, she stabbed a note to the chest of the baby she cut out of your brother's girlfriend's stomach."

Rita cringed at the memory. "I know. I remember. Sneed told me everything."

"Did he tell you what the note said?" "No, but I'm assuming you will."

"It said something about "the ten." We believe it's a reference to ten

submarines that are currently being used by the Sinaloa and Los Zetas cartels to get their dope into the U.S. Word is those cartels are now taking orders from Alexus."

"What else did this little note say?" Rita was struggling to repress her fear of the Mexican drug cartels. It was a fear that had been instilled in her by the sadistic Jennifer Costilla, a fear that would stay with her all her life.

"It also spoke briefly of the other Costillas— Papi's distant relatives. They're supposedly "the righteous ones." I think they're only joining ISIS to gain control of the drug trafficking."

"I don't know anything about drugs," Rita lied. She knew her daughter was a cartel boss, and Neal knew it, too. But admitting it wasn't easy for Rita. She was still in denial.

"I didn't say you knew anything. I said Alexus knows."

"What does this have to do with me? I don't wanna hear this crap, Neal. I'm already stressed half to death worrying about Alexus and my grandbabies. You're not making it any better. Tell me something good sometimes. I'm sick of the drama."

Neal draped an arm around her shoulders and squeezed her against his side.

He glanced at the television. As always with Rita, it was a Denzel Washington movie. "Stash House."

"You're obsessed with that guy, aren't you?" "He's a great actor."

"I'm not trying to hurt you, Rita Mae. I'm sorry if I came off that way. It wasn't my intention."

A moment of silence ensued. He rubbed her shoulder. She read another Bible verse.

"I sure hope Blake doesn't act a fool about you bringing that guy here," Rita said finally. "You know he's missing a few screws. He'll kill that man."

"Blake belongs in prison, Rita Mae, and you know it. He's a killer." "He's innocent until proven guilty. That's the law, isn't it?"

"Not when it comes to thugs like Blake. He's scum, Rita Mae. You

hear me? Scum. He killed two of my officers. I know it for a fact. Might not be able to prove it, but it's true. I wish he'd do us all a favor and just admit it. Get it over with, you know?"

"Stop it, Neal."

"Be honest with yourself, Rita. He's a scumbag and he deserves the needle. He murdered two of my of-ficers in cold blood. We may not be able to prove it but it's the truth and you know it. Alexus needs a good man, not a criminal. Blake is a—"

A knock at the bedroom door silenced him. "Grandma?" It was Savaria.

"Yes, baby?" Rita said.

"Is my daddy coming here to this house?"

"I don't know yet, Vari," Rita said, giving Neal a cold stare. "If he doesn't make it in tonight he'll proba-bly be here in the morning."

Vari's sigh could be heard through the door. "Okay. Goodnight, Grandma."

Rita continued her icy stare until Neal shifted his attention to the television. While watching the movie, he tried to figure out a way to get Blake tried and convicted for the heinous murders of two MCPD officers and several others that had occurred in 2010.

He was determined to make it happen.

King Rio

Chapter 45

Kita had one of the sexiest moans Blake had ever heard.

Holding on to her hips and thrusting his rigid dick in and out of her warm, gripping pussy, he thought back to when he used to fuck her at that same mansion and concluded that those were among his best memories.

The tequila had him buzzed and horny; Kita's pussy was just what he needed. Now he wasn't thinking about Alexus or what she might be doing on the secluded island. Fuck it, he thought, if Alexus is having fun, then it's only right that I have some fun, too.

Biggs and Shay must have been fucking somewhere near the mansion's rear patio doors, because Blake could clearly hear Shay's passionate screams.

Kita's moans were just as loud.

"Told you I missed you, didn't I?" Blake asked. "Still think I'm lyin'?

Hm?"

All Kita could do was moan as he dug in with deep, pounding thrusts, rubbing her lower back, and holding a thumb inside her asshole. Every minute or so she shook and trembled in orgasm, but he went on remorselessly.

Then he did what he knew she was waiting on: he pulled out of her juicy pussy and slipped his dick into her ass, just like he used to, and the snug feeling almost made him come.

But he didn't.

He slowed his pace, but only long enough to regain control of himself.

Then he began fucking her asshole just as roughly as he'd pounded her pussy.

"Yes...yes...yes...ooooooh," she moaned, holding her big brown butt cheeks apart with both hands and gazing back at him as he plunged in and out, in and out.

His iPhone 6 was ringing on the bar— he'd left it there between the Patrón bottle and his Mac-11 — but he wasn't going to answer it until he was finished with Kita.

She turned over on her back. He sucked and tongued her clitoris until she tremored in orgasm again, then spit on her asshole and slid back into it.

He looked up to the dark, star-filled Miami sky and relaxed. There was nothing to be worried about, he decided. The gunplay with T-Walk and Chief Keef was over. The US government was already bombing ISIS compounds in Central America and carrying out raids on suspected terrorists there in the States. All that was left for Blake to do was chill and raise his children.

And love his wife.

He pulled out abruptly, removed the rubber, and was tempted by his vows to Alexus to put his perilous magic stick away.

But then Kita turned and slurped him right into her mouth.

She sucked him for another ten minutes or so and he doused her tongue with ropes of semen...just as three men with hoods drawn tight over their faces came running out from the side of the mansion.

They aimed guns at Blake— an AK-47, a Tec, and a handgun with a balefully long clip.

Blake had no choice but to run toward the bar where his gun was laying, and he tried vehemently.

Gunfire erupted.

Chapter 46

"Don't touch me," Alexus said in the sternest tone she could summon.

She stood stiff with her back to the closed door and flicked on the light. Displaying a warm smile, she shoved Manchild onto the bed with one hand and dialed Enrique on her iPhone with the other.

"Get in here," she said, and ended the call abruptly. "Who was that?" Manchild asked.

Alexus gave no reply. She stood there and stared at him for a long moment. He took it as foreplay and began massaging his manhood.

"Get over here," he said.

"I'm a lot like my father was, you know that?" She opened her large Chanel shoulder bag and pulled out her cherished gold-plated .50-caliber Desert Eagle.

Manchild's eyes became as wide as saucers.

"I know who you are," Alexus said, flicking on the red laser sighting and settling the dot on the tip of his nose. She regarded him with a harsh, accusatory glare. "You're not the real Manchild. The real Manchild from Forty-second and Post Road in Indianapolis is a big black guy with life in prison. You stole his identity. I'm wondering if it was to get close to me? Or my husband? Who put you up to this?"

"I...I don't know what you mean..."

"See? That kinda talk right there. You ain't no dope boy. You're a rat.

Who sent you?"

Just then, Enrique knocked at the bedroom door and let himself in.

He already had his golden AK-47 raised.

Fire belched forth from the assault rifle's barrel.

Alexus was briefly stunned by the large bloody holes that appeared in Manchild's muscular brown chest.

Then she walked forward, stood over him, and put a bullet in his forehead that knocked the back of his skull and all of his brains onto the clean brown Louis Vuitton blanket.

Several of the girls screamed from out in the hallway.

"Oh, my God, somebody's shooting," Alexus heard Melonie say. "He was a fed," Enrique said. "Work-ing with Neal and that FBI agent. They're trying to take Blake down. You too, but they're more focused on getting him for killing those cops first. He's a gangster billionaire who allegedly killed two of theirs. You know they've got zero tolerance for that." He unsnapped a pocket on his belt and took out a golden hunting knife. "You want his head?"

"You know I do."

Enrique was no newbie to the beheading game. It barely took him thirty seconds, and by then Britney, Melonie, and Porsche had gotten brave enough to venture up to the door.

The trio gasped in unison.

"Sneed can't fuck with us," Alexus said. She kicked the door shut on the spectators. "The FBI has been accepting my money. The CIA is still with us. Indicting me would bring down the entire US government. They want Blake." She glanced at the dripping head as Enrique held it by the scalp. "Bag that up and send it to Sneed. And send somebody up to kill Neal Miller. I don't care what my mom has to say about it. She'll live."

Enrique nodded and ordered the hit on his smartphone. "Done."

"Okay...now get an eye on Blake. I wanna know where he's at and who he's with."

"Meant to tell you about that before I shot this rat," Enrique said. "Tell me what?"

"He's at the mansion he had when you split from him a few years ago. He lost us on the highway but we found him with a drone." "What's he doing there?"

Enrique paused for an uncomfortably long moment. Alexus grew hotter and hotter by the second. "He's talking to Kita—" "He fuckin' that bitch?"

Enrique nodded a solemn yes. "No need to get mad, though. He's shot to pieces. Some guys just shot him up."

"What?"
"Yeah, and I don't think he'll survive this one."

King Rio

Chapter 47

The main reason Rita had purchased the private island was for safety and security. There were over 2,200 strategically positioned cameras spread across the 986-acre island, and she could access all of them from her iPad.

At the sound of gunfire, Rita snatched up the iPad from the bedside table and hopped out of bed. "My grandbabies," she murmured fearfully, and ran from the room.

She found King and Vari fast asleep in their bedrooms before she located Alexus and Enrique standing in a bedroom, seemingly talking.

Alexus looked frantic.

Rita was just about to beep in on the room's intercom when she noticed the headless body on the bed.

"What's going on?" Neal asked from behind her.

She turned and saw that he had his police-issue Glock 27 in hand.

He was in a half-crouch, both hands on the gun, glancing every which way.

Two of Alexus's bodyguards rushed up the glass staircase with their submachine guns drawn.

Neal turned his gun on them.

"Easy, easy, easy," said one bodyguard. "We're only making sure Rita's okay. Someone just tried attacking Alexus."

"Who was it?" Neal asked.

"Will you please lower the weapon?"

"I ain't gotta lower a mothafuckin' thing till I deem—"

The sound suppressor on the bodyguard's gun hardly made a whistle, but Neal's gun let out a stentorian bark.

Neal hit the floor with a bullet hole in his chin and another beneath his right eye.

Rita screamed as he hit the floor.

Chapter 48

Alexus was a nervous wreck during the flight from the Caribbean island, and she became even more nervous when she and Enrique boarded a helicopter from the airport to Mt. Sinai Medical Center where Blake was being treated.

She got the news as soon as she entered the hospital. A doctor with a thick gray moustache delivered it to her in the gentlest of tones.

"Blake King was shot seven times. We believe he's going to make it..."

Alexus became dizzy very suddenly, and for the first time ever, she fainted.

King Rio

Chapter 49

Two days later Trintino "T-Walk" Walkson stepped out of his Miami mansion wearing a victorious smile over a tailored Armani suit. As always, Ashley was at his side, dressed to impress in a one-shouldered white Gucci dress and Louboutin pumps. The sky blue Phantom he'd recently purchased specifically to commute to and from work on sets of the MTN reality shows he'd created waited for him.

"You should've talked to Cup about that hit on Blake," she said. "Y'all were supposed to be working together, getting the dope first. At least that's what you told me."

"I don't care about that hit. Fuck Blake. I hope he dies for real this time. Let the nigga go out like Pac since he wanna be such a rap star. It still turned out perfect for us. Alexus gave me that gig back. I'll be making at least a hundred million every year. We're set, baby. We're set for life."

"I love you so much, T-Walk. I really do. We should set our wedding date for—"

Ashley gasped as a mist of blood and brain matter sprayed onto her beautiful chocolate face.

T-Walk thumped to the ground with a nickel-sized hole in his left brow.

His fiancée screamed out in horror when she realized he'd been shot.

To Be Continued...
The Cocaine Princess 7
Coming Soon

King Rio

Lock Down Publications and Ca$h Presents assisted
publishing packages.

BASIC PACKAGE $499
Editing
Cover Design
Formatting

UPGRADED PACKAGE $800
Typing
Editing
Cover Design
Formatting

ADVANCE PACKAGE $1,200
Typing
Editing
Cover Design
Formatting
Copyright registration
Proofreading
Upload book to Amazon

LDP SUPREME PACKAGE $1,500
Typing
Editing
Cover Design
Formatting
Copyright registration
Proofreading
Set up Amazon account
Upload book to Amazon
Advertise on LDP Amazon and Facebook page

***Other services available upon request. Additional charges may apply
Lock Down Publications
P.O. Box 944
Stockbridge, GA 30281-9998
Phone # 470 303-9761

Submission Guideline

Submit the first three chapters of your completed manuscript to ldpsubmissions@gmail.com, subject line: Your book's title. The manuscript must be in a .doc file and sent as an attachment. Document should be in Times New Roman, double spaced and in size 12 font. Also, provide your synopsis and full contact information. If sending multiple submissions, they must each be in a separate email.

Have a story but no way to send it electronically? You can still submit to LDP/Ca$h Presents. Send in the first three chapters, written or typed, of your completed manuscript to:

LDP: Submissions Dept
Po Box 944
Stockbridge, Ga 30281

DO NOT send original manuscript. Must be a duplicate.

Provide your synopsis and a cover letter containing your full contact information.

Thanks for considering LDP and Ca$h Presents.

<u>NEW RELEASES</u>

IF YOU CROSS ME ONCE 2 by ANTHONY FIELDS

PILLOW PRINCESS by S. HAWKINS

LOYALTY IS EVERYTHING 2 by MOLOTTI

THE COCAINE PRINCESS 6 by KING RIO

King Rio

STRAIGHT BEAST MODE III

De'Kari

KINGPIN KILLAZ IV

STREET KINGS III

PAID IN BLOOD III

CARTEL KILLAZ IV

DOPE GODS III

Hood Rich

SINS OF A HUSTLA II

ASAD

YAYO V

Bred In The Game 2

S. Allen

THE STREETS WILL TALK II

By Yolanda Moore

SON OF A DOPE FIEND III

HEAVEN GOT A GHETTO II

SKI MASK MONEY II

By Renta

LOYALTY AIN'T PROMISED III

By Keith Williams

I'M NOTHING WITHOUT HIS LOVE II

SINS OF A THUG II

TO THE THUG I LOVED BEFORE II

IN A HUSTLER I TRUST II

By Monet Dragun

QUIET MONEY IV

EXTENDED CLIP III

THUG LIFE IV

By **Trai'Quan**

King Rio

THE STREETS MADE ME IV

By **Larry D. Wright**

IF YOU CROSS ME ONCE III

ANGEL V

By **Anthony Fields**

THE STREETS WILL NEVER CLOSE IV

By **K'ajji**

HARD AND RUTHLESS III

KILLA KOUNTY IV

By **Khufu**

MONEY GAME III

By **Smoove Dolla**

JACK BOYS VS DOPE BOYS IV

A GANGSTA'S QUR'AN V

COKE GIRLZ II

COKE BOYS II

LIFE OF A SAVAGE V

CHI'RAQ GANGSTAS V

By **Romell Tukes**

MURDA WAS THE CASE III

Elijah R. Freeman

THE STREETS NEVER LET GO III

By **Robert Baptiste**

AN UNFORESEEN LOVE IV

BABY, I'M WINTERTIME COLD III

By **Meesha**

QUEEN OF THE ZOO III

By **Black Migo**

VICIOUS LOYALTY III

By Kingpen

A GANGSTA'S PAIN III

By J-Blunt

CONFESSIONS OF A JACKBOY III

By Nicholas Lock

GRIMEY WAYS III

By Ray Vinci

KING KILLA II

By Vincent "Vitto" Holloway

BETRAYAL OF A THUG III

By Fre$h

THE MURDER QUEENS III

By Michael Gallon

THE BIRTH OF A GANGSTER III

By Delmont Player

TREAL LOVE II

By Le'Monica Jackson

FOR THE LOVE OF BLOOD III

By Jamel Mitchell

RAN OFF ON DA PLUG II

By Paper Boi Rari

HOOD CONSIGLIERE III

By Keese

PRETTY GIRLS DO NASTY THINGS II

By Nicole Goosby

PROTÉGÉ OF A LEGEND II

By Corey Robinson

IT'S JUST ME AND YOU II

By Ah'Million

BORN IN THE GRAVE III

King Rio

By Self Made Tay
FOREVER GANGSTA III
By Adrian Dulan
GORILLAZ IN THE TRENCHES II
By SayNoMore
THE COCAINE PRINCESS VII
By King Rio
CRIME BOSS II
Playa Ray
LOYALTY IS EVERYTHING III
Molotti
HERE TODAY GONE TOMORROW II
By Fly Rock
REAL G'S MOVE IN SILENCE II
By Von Diesel

Available Now

RESTRAINING ORDER **I & II**
By **CA$H & Coffee**
LOVE KNOWS NO BOUNDARIES **I II & III**
By **Coffee**
RAISED AS A GOON I, II, III & IV
BRED BY THE SLUMS I, II, III
BLAST FOR ME I & II
ROTTEN TO THE CORE I II III
A BRONX TALE I, II, III

DUFFLE BAG CARTEL I II III IV V VI

HEARTLESS GOON I II III IV V

A SAVAGE DOPEBOY I II

DRUG LORDS I II III

CUTTHROAT MAFIA I II

KING OF THE TRENCHES

By **Ghost**

LAY IT DOWN **I & II**

LAST OF A DYING BREED I II

BLOOD STAINS OF A SHOTTA I & II III

By **Jamaica**

LOYAL TO THE GAME I II III

LIFE OF SIN I, II III

By **TJ & Jelissa**

BLOODY COMMAS I & II

SKI MASK CARTEL I II & III

KING OF NEW YORK I II,III IV V

RISE TO POWER I II III

COKE KINGS I II III IV V

BORN HEARTLESS I II III IV

KING OF THE TRAP I II

By **T.J. Edwards**

IF LOVING HIM IS WRONG...I & II

LOVE ME EVEN WHEN IT HURTS I II III

By **Jelissa**

WHEN THE STREETS CLAP BACK I & II III

THE HEART OF A SAVAGE I II III IV

MONEY MAFIA I II

LOYAL TO THE SOIL I II III

By **Jibril Williams**

King Rio

A DISTINGUISHED THUG STOLE MY HEART I II & III

LOVE SHOULDN'T HURT I II III IV

RENEGADE BOYS I II III IV

PAID IN KARMA I II III

SAVAGE STORMS I II III

AN UNFORESEEN LOVE I II III

BABY, I'M WINTERTIME COLD I II

By **Meesha**

A GANGSTER'S CODE I &, II III

A GANGSTER'S SYN I II III

THE SAVAGE LIFE I II III

CHAINED TO THE STREETS I II III

BLOOD ON THE MONEY I II III

A GANGSTA'S PAIN I II

By J-Blunt

PUSH IT TO THE LIMIT

By **Bre' Hayes**

BLOOD OF A BOSS **I, II, III, IV, V**

SHADOWS OF THE GAME

TRAP BASTARD

By **Askari**

THE STREETS BLEED MURDER **I, II & III**

THE HEART OF A GANGSTA I II& III

By **Jerry Jackson**

CUM FOR ME I II III IV V VI VII VIII

An **LDP Erotica Collaboration**

BRIDE OF A HUSTLA **I II & II**

THE FETTI GIRLS **I, II& III**

CORRUPTED BY A GANGSTA I, II III, IV

BLINDED BY HIS LOVE

THE PRICE YOU PAY FOR LOVE I, II ,III

DOPE GIRL MAGIC I II III

By **Destiny Skai**

WHEN A GOOD GIRL GOES BAD

By **Adrienne**

THE COST OF LOYALTY I II III

By Kweli

A GANGSTER'S REVENGE **I II III & IV**

THE BOSS MAN'S DAUGHTERS I II III IV V

A SAVAGE LOVE **I & II**

BAE BELONGS TO ME I II

A HUSTLER'S DECEIT I, II, III

WHAT BAD BITCHES DO I, II, III

SOUL OF A MONSTER I II III

KILL ZONE

A DOPE BOY'S QUEEN I II III

TIL DEATH

By **Aryanna**

A KINGPIN'S AMBITON

A KINGPIN'S AMBITION **II**

I MURDER FOR THE DOUGH

By **Ambitious**

TRUE SAVAGE I II III IV V VI VII

DOPE BOY MAGIC I, II, III

MIDNIGHT CARTEL I II III

CITY OF KINGZ I II

NIGHTMARE ON SILENT AVE

THE PLUG OF LIL MEXICO II

CLASSIC CITY

By **Chris Green**

King Rio

A DOPEBOY'S PRAYER

By **Eddie "Wolf" Lee**

THE KING CARTEL **I, II & III**

By **Frank Gresham**

THESE NIGGAS AIN'T LOYAL **I, II & III**

By **Nikki Tee**

GANGSTA SHYT **I II &III**

By **CATO**

THE ULTIMATE BETRAYAL

By **Phoenix**

BOSS'N UP **I , II & III**

By **Royal Nicole**

I LOVE YOU TO DEATH

By **Destiny J**

I RIDE FOR MY HITTA

I STILL RIDE FOR MY HITTA

By **Misty Holt**

LOVE & CHASIN' PAPER

By **Qay Crockett**

TO DIE IN VAIN

SINS OF A HUSTLA

By **ASAD**

BROOKLYN HUSTLAZ

By **Boogsy Morina**

BROOKLYN ON LOCK I & II

By **Sonovia**

GANGSTA CITY

By **Teddy Duke**

A DRUG KING AND HIS DIAMOND I & II III

A DOPEMAN'S RICHES

HER MAN, MINE'S TOO I, II
CASH MONEY HO'S
THE WIFEY I USED TO BE I II
PRETTY GIRLS DO NASTY THINGS
By Nicole Goosby
TRAPHOUSE KING **I II & III**
KINGPIN KILLAZ I II III
STREET KINGS I II
PAID IN BLOOD **I II**
CARTEL KILLAZ I II III
DOPE GODS I II
By **Hood Rich**
LIPSTICK KILLAH **I, II, III**
CRIME OF PASSION I II & III
FRIEND OR FOE I II III
By **Mimi**
STEADY MOBBN' **I, II, III**
THE STREETS STAINED MY SOUL I II III
By **Marcellus Allen**
WHO SHOT YA **I, II, III**
SON OF A DOPE FIEND I II
HEAVEN GOT A GHETTO
SKI MASK MONEY
Renta
GORILLAZ IN THE BAY **I II III IV**
TEARS OF A GANGSTA I II
3X KRAZY I II
STRAIGHT BEAST MODE I II
DE'KARI
TRIGGADALE I II III

King Rio

MURDAROBER WAS THE CASE I II

Elijah R. Freeman

GOD BLESS THE TRAPPERS I, II, III

THESE SCANDALOUS STREETS I, II, III

FEAR MY GANGSTA I, II, III IV, V

THESE STREETS DON'T LOVE NOBODY I, II

BURY ME A G I, II, III, IV, V

A GANGSTA'S EMPIRE I, II, III, IV

THE DOPEMAN'S BODYGAURD I II

THE REALEST KILLAZ I II III

THE LAST OF THE OGS I II III

Tranay Adams

THE STREETS ARE CALLING

Duquie Wilson

MARRIED TO A BOSS I II III

By Destiny Skai & Chris Green

KINGZ OF THE GAME I II III IV V VI

CRIME BOSS

Playa Ray

SLAUGHTER GANG I II III

RUTHLESS HEART I II III

By Willie Slaughter

FUK SHYT

By Blakk Diamond

DON'T F#CK WITH MY HEART I II

By Linnea

ADDICTED TO THE DRAMA I II III

IN THE ARM OF HIS BOSS II

By Jamila

YAYO I II III IV

A SHOOTER'S AMBITION I II

BRED IN THE GAME

By S. Allen

TRAP GOD I II III

RICH $AVAGE I II III

MONEY IN THE GRAVE I II III

By Martell Troublesome Bolden

FOREVER GANGSTA I II

GLOCKS ON SATIN SHEETS I II

By Adrian Dulan

TOE TAGZ I II III IV

LEVELS TO THIS SHYT I II

IT'S JUST ME AND YOU

By Ah'Million

KINGPIN DREAMS I II III

RAN OFF ON DA PLUG

By Paper Boi Rari

CONFESSIONS OF A GANGSTA I II III IV

CONFESSIONS OF A JACKBOY I II

By Nicholas Lock

I'M NOTHING WITHOUT HIS LOVE

SINS OF A THUG

TO THE THUG I LOVED BEFORE

A GANGSTA SAVED XMAS

IN A HUSTLER I TRUST

By Monet Dragun

CAUGHT UP IN THE LIFE I II III

THE STREETS NEVER LET GO I II

By Robert Baptiste

NEW TO THE GAME I II III

King Rio

MONEY, MURDER & MEMORIES I II III

By **Malik D. Rice**

LIFE OF A SAVAGE I II III IV

A GANGSTA'S QUR'AN I II III IV

MURDA SEASON I II III

GANGLAND CARTEL I II III

CHI'RAQ GANGSTAS I II III IV

KILLERS ON ELM STREET I II III

JACK BOYZ N DA BRONX I II III

A DOPEBOY'S DREAM I II III

JACK BOYS VS DOPE BOYS I II III

COKE GIRLZ

COKE BOYS

By **Romell Tukes**

LOYALTY AIN'T PROMISED I II

By **Keith Williams**

QUIET MONEY I II III

THUG LIFE I II III

EXTENDED CLIP I II

A GANGSTA'S PARADISE

By **Trai'Quan**

THE STREETS MADE ME I II III

By **Larry D. Wright**

THE ULTIMATE SACRIFICE I, II, III, IV, V, VI

KHADIFI

IF YOU CROSS ME ONCE I II

ANGEL I II III IV

IN THE BLINK OF AN EYE

By **Anthony Fields**

THE LIFE OF A HOOD STAR

By Ca$h & Rashia Wilson
THE STREETS WILL NEVER CLOSE I II III
By K'ajji
CREAM I II III
THE STREETS WILL TALK
By Yolanda Moore
NIGHTMARES OF A HUSTLA I II III
By King Dream
CONCRETE KILLA I II III
VICIOUS LOYALTY I II
By Kingpen
HARD AND RUTHLESS I II
MOB TOWN 251
THE BILLIONAIRE BENTLEYS I II III
REAL G'S MOVE IN SILENCE
By Von Diesel
GHOST MOB
Stilloan Robinson
MOB TIES I II III IV V VI
SOUL OF A HUSTLER, HEART OF A KILLER
GORILLAZ IN THE TRENCHES
By SayNoMore
BODYMORE MURDERLAND I II III
THE BIRTH OF A GANGSTER I II
By Delmont Player
FOR THE LOVE OF A BOSS
By C. D. Blue
MOBBED UP I II III IV
THE BRICK MAN I II III IV V
THE COCAINE PRINCESS I II III IV V VI

King Rio

By King Rio
KILLA KOUNTY I II III IV
By Khufu
MONEY GAME I II
By Smoove Dolla
A GANGSTA'S KARMA I II III
By FLAME
KING OF THE TRENCHES I II III
by **GHOST & TRANAY ADAMS**
QUEEN OF THE ZOO I II
By **Black Migo**
GRIMEY WAYS I II
By Ray Vinci
XMAS WITH AN ATL SHOOTER
By Ca$h & Destiny Skai
KING KILLA
By Vincent "Vitto" Holloway
BETRAYAL OF A THUG I II
By Fre$h
THE MURDER QUEENS I II
By Michael Gallon
TREAL LOVE
By Le'Monica Jackson
FOR THE LOVE OF BLOOD I II
By Jamel Mitchell
HOOD CONSIGLIERE I II
By Keese
PROTÉGÉ OF A LEGEND
By Corey Robinson
BORN IN THE GRAVE I II

By Self Made Tay

MOAN IN MY MOUTH

By XTASY

TORN BETWEEN A GANGSTER AND A GENTLEMAN

By J-BLUNT & Miss Kim

LOYALTY IS EVERYTHING I II

Molotti

HERE TODAY GONE TOMORROW

By Fly Rock

PILLOW PRINCESS

By S. Hawkins

King Rio

<u>BOOKS BY LDP'S CEO, CA$H</u>

TRUST IN NO MAN

TRUST IN NO MAN 2

TRUST IN NO MAN 3

BONDED BY BLOOD

SHORTY GOT A THUG

THUGS CRY

THUGS CRY 2

THUGS CRY 3

TRUST NO BITCH

TRUST NO BITCH 2

TRUST NO BITCH 3

TIL MY CASKET DROPS

RESTRAINING ORDER

RESTRAINING ORDER 2

IN LOVE WITH A CONVICT

LIFE OF A HOOD STAR

XMAS WITH AN ATL SHOOTER

The Cocaine Princess 6

www.ingramcontent.com/pod-product-compliance
Lightning Source LLC
Chambersburg PA
CBHW070755280626
47162CB00016B/1063